"I will kill this girl immediately!"

The man's high-pitched voice threatened to shatter the eardrums of everyone in the Learjet. "You fill a suitcase with old magazines and think we will not open it before we release the woman?"

"Well, Moe," Bolan said, holding the mike up to his mouth again, "it was all I could think of to do. We didn't *have* a million dollars to give you." Now was the moment of truth. The woman would live or die.

"You have not heard the last from us," Moe screamed. "And the blood of this young woman is on your hands!"

The radio suddenly went silent.

Bolan saw a woman wearing a red dress—her hands and feet tied together—being shoved out of the Cessna just below them.

"Parachute!" he yelled at the top of his voice as he snapped open his seat belt.

With the unopened parachute clenched in his fist, Bolan never even broke stride as he raced out the door and into the open air thousands of feet above the earth.

MACK BOLAN ®

The Executioner

The Executioner®
Don Pendleton's
FACE OF TERROR

A GOLD EAGLE BOOK FROM
WORLDWIDE®

TORONTO • NEW YORK • LONDON
AMSTERDAM • PARIS • SYDNEY • HAMBURG
STOCKHOLM • ATHENS • TOKYO • MILAN
MADRID • WARSAW • BUDAPEST • AUCKLAND

Recycling programs
for this product may
not exist in your area.

First edition February 2009

ISBN-13: 978-0-373-64363-9
ISBN-10: · 0-373-64363-2

Special thanks and acknowledgment to
Jerry VanCook for his contribution to this work.

FACE OF TERROR

Printed in U.S.A.

What is left when honor is lost?
                    —Publilius Syrus: Sententiae
                         1st century B.C.

There is no greater dishonor than when a soldier
turns traitor. I will make sure those traitors cannot
win.

                                        —Mack Bolan

THE
MACK BOLAN
LEGEND

Nothing less than a war could have fashioned the destiny of the man called Mack Bolan. Bolan earned the Executioner title in the jungle hell of Vietnam.

But this soldier also wore another name—Sergeant Mercy. He was so tagged because of the compassion he showed to wounded comrades-in-arms and Vietnamese civilians.

Mack Bolan's second tour of duty ended prematurely when he was given emergency leave to return home and bury his family, victims of the Mob. Then he declared a one-man war against the Mafia.

He confronted the Families head-on from coast to coast, and soon a hope of victory began to appear. But Bolan had broken society's every rule. That same society started gunning for this elusive warrior—to no avail.

So Bolan was offered amnesty to work within the system against terrorism. This time, as an employee of Uncle Sam, Bolan became Colonel John Phoenix. With a command center at Stony Man Farm in Virginia, he and his new allies—Able Team and Phoenix Force—waged relentless war on a new adversary: the KGB.

But when his one true love, April Rose, died at the hands of the Soviet terror machine, Bolan severed all ties with Establishment authority.

Now, after a lengthy lone-wolf struggle and much soul-searching, the Executioner has agreed to enter an "arm's-length" alliance with his government once more, reserving the right to pursue personal missions in his Everlasting War.

Prologue

Susan McDonald could not have been happier.

As she stood proudly behind her shelf at the teller's window, she felt the hard granite press lightly against her swelling abdomen. The baby—ultrasound images had already assured her husband and her that it was a boy—was kicking lightly. Susan's doctor had warned her that soon he'd be kicking like a professional soccer player, that he'd wake her up at night and make her jump in the middle of sentences.

The baby was almost the only thing she could think of these days. Almost. But the other thing was too ghastly to think about, and so unlikely to happen at her branch of the First Federal Bank that she easily pushed it to the back of her mind.

Frank Dutton, the loan officer in charge of this branch office, walked to the front door, where several customers waited to conduct their early-morning banking. Frank selected a key from the large ring he'd produced from his pocket, unlocked the door, then held it open as the customers filed inside.

"Good morning, Mabel. Hello, Tim. Hey, Charlie, how's the book coming?"

Frank knew every regular customer by name, which was one of the reasons the First Federal Bank's outpost on South Western had more customers, and did more business, than any of the other branches.

Susan looked down the row of smiling women's faces at the other tellers' windows. Most were blond and all were beautiful. That was another reason the customers—at least the males—never seemed to switch banks.

The customer Frank had called Charlie limped toward Susan, leaning on his cane. He had a white beard beneath his well-worn brown fedora, and a tie-dyed T-shirt bearing a picture of Janis Joplin riding a motorcycle covered his chest. Susan knew he was a veteran of the Vietnam War, a former cop and still taught self-defense clinics on occasion. He'd recently taken a medical retirement from the police department because arthritis had set into almost every joint he had— most of which had been broken or dislocated at one time or another during his life of adventure. Now he wrote articles for magazines and was working on a book about his experiences in Southeast Asia.

Susan's mind flashed back to the one problem that even her baby couldn't force from her mind, and she knew the sight of Charlie limping forward had forced it to her consciousness. A rash of violent bank robberies had plagued almost all of the major cities surrounding Chicago. And it appeared to be the work of the same gang. The police suspected that the robbers were actually members of an Arabic terrorist cell. Any people inside the bank during the robberies who showed even the slightest sign of resistance were immediately murdered.

Charlie dropped a checkbook on the counter and began endorsing several checks. "Morning, Susie," he greeted. He passed the checks and deposit slips through the hole at the bottom of the glass that separated them, and was about to speak when the front door suddenly burst into flying shards of glass.

Everyone inside the bank froze.

Susan watched in horror as, one by one, five men dressed in multicolored Army camou outfits with black ski masks covering their faces crunched over the glass inside the bank.

Susan and the others were still glued into position as Charlie produced a silver-colored gun from beneath his T-shirt and turned to face the robbers. He got off three quick shots— all of which looked like they'd hit their targets in the chest by the robbers' reactions—before another of the men turned some kind of machine gun on Charlie and shot him three times. One of the bullets made the elderly customer drop his pistol, but he suddenly pulled a thin sword out of his cane and staggered toward the men in the Army shirts and pants.

It took only one more round to drop Charlie to the floor.

Susan screamed, which made the other tellers scream. Then the loan officers and customers began screaming, too.

The five robbers were trying to shout over the shrieks in some kind of foreign language. It was probably Arabic, Susan thought. She was about to drop down to her knees behind the counter when one of the men switched to heavily accented English. "Do not move! If you do as I say, no one else will be harmed!"

Susan's eyes darted back to the three men Charlie had shot, and she saw that they were still on their feet. Bulletproof vests, she thought. She remembered that some robbers in California had worn them a few years ago, and the police had had a terrible time trying to stop them.

The man who had spoken in heavily accented English now fired a burst into the ceiling. "Shut up!" he yelled. "Shut up now, all of you, or I will kill each and every one!"

Suddenly, the main lobby of the bank went silent. Susan had planned to drop to her knees a moment earlier, but now those same knees made the decision for her. She sank to the tile floor as if she'd been given a local anesthetic in both legs, and had to force herself to slide in beneath the counter.

From where she now hid, Susan heard the same voice ordering the tellers to come around to the front lobby. Each one who passed her looked down to where she hid. Some were crying. Others were in shock.

Susan realized that if any of the bank robbers came back behind the counter they would easily find her. But the time to surrender had come and gone. Something in her heart told Susan that if she slid out and got to her feet now, she'd be immediately killed.

And so would her baby.

Behind her, through the thin wall, Susan heard the man speaking English order everyone to the carpet. A few seconds later, she heard him speaking in that strange tongue again. A moment after he stopped, she heard the sounds of doors opening and closing from the part of the bank that held the loan officers' offices and supply rooms.

The robbers were looking for anyone who had hidden, Susan knew, and that realization made her heart pound so hard she feared she might have a miscarriage.

The half door that separated the lobby from the tellers' area swung open, and two of the men in Army clothes appeared in front of Susan. She pulled her knees tighter against her chest, but the baby inside her kept her from getting her legs out of sight. The two men walked past her and, unless the stress was causing her to hallucinate, neither of them noticed her feet sticking out from under the counter.

The men headed for the vault in the back of the bank. They disappeared for a few minutes, then reappeared at the doorway leading back to the tellers' area. One of them was looking at his wristwatch. A little later, an explosion sounded from the vault room.

Another man wearing a ski mask now hurried through the swing door and followed the first two back into the vault room. They spoke excitedly in their foreign tongue, then came back carrying large cotton money bags.

It took them three trips to get it all.

Behind her again now, Susan could hear the crunch of the broken glass beneath their boots as they began carrying the money out to whatever vehicle awaited them. Then, evidently finished and ready to leave, Susan heard the same man who had done all of the talking speak again. "Allahu Akhbar!" he shouted at the top of his lungs. "Death to all infidels!"

Then the room erupted with the explosions of all of the men's machine guns, and Susan closed her eyes again and prayed. *Dear God,* she mouthed silently. Please spare the life of my child if not mine. Then she began to cry.

She was still crying five minutes later when the police arrived. It took a good minute after that for her to pry her eyes open and face what had happened.

Inside her belly, her baby boy was kicking like a well-trained rooster at a cockfight.

They had received the exact location from DEA Special
Agent Rick Jessup's informant only minutes earlier. Which
meant they had mere minutes to reach the site of the cocaine
transaction before the deal would be over and the drug
pushers gone.

Mack Bolan, aka the Executioner, continued to floor the accelerator of the civilian-market Hummer. It was not the kind of
vehicle he'd expected to find waiting for him when he'd arrived
in Guyman, Oklahoma, earlier that morning.

With its bright yellow paint job, the only advantage it might
have was that it stood out so much that no one in his right mind
would believe any police agency would have the audacity to use
it as an undercover vehicle.

But Bolan knew that would be a short-lived advantage. The
bright Hummer might work fine for inner-city surveillance,
but as soon as any action started, that advantage would disappear in a cloud of smoke.

Gun smoke.

Then again, Bolan had learned to work within the limitations
of the equipment he had on hand, and he did not intend to quit
doing so now.

The stakes in this game were simply too high to fold now.

Ever since Jessup's informant indicated that a large cocaine
deal was about to go down in the Oklahoma panhandle, Bolan
had dressed and played the part of a wealthy Southwestern
businessman. Both he and Agent Jessup wore exotic-skinned
boots—Jessup's were ostrich, Bolan's anteater—carefully

pressed blue jeans and colorful Western shirts with bolo ties of silver and turquoise.

Bolan continued to press the Hummer to its maximum speed while Jessup studied the hand-drawn map he had made while talking to his informant over the phone. "I think it's the next turn," he told the Executioner. "Yeah, there's the motel my guy mentioned." He pointed at a small set of brick buildings on the right side of the road. "Out in the middle of nowhere just like he said. Almost exactly halfway between Guyman and Boise City. That means we turn right the next time we see dirt."

The Hummer flashed past the motel and sped on.

Oklahoma's panhandle was known for its flatness, and the eye could indeed see for miles. The terrain was mostly prairie, with a few occasional wheat fields.

Not the usual sort of place radical Islamic terrorists or mafiosi would pick to do a drug deal. Then again, they might be working off the same sort of psychology the Executioner was using with the Hummer—picking a place so bereft of privacy that no lawmen were likely to even consider it.

In other words, hiding in plain sight.

Bolan saw the quarter-section road ahead and felt his eyebrows lower in concentration as he slowed. Middle-Eastern terrorists doing business with old-school Phoenix mafiosi didn't constitute an average run-of-the-mill dope deal, either. But Bolan had seen stranger alliances form when there was a buck to be made.

Twelve-thirty p.m., which was what the Executioner's watch read at the moment, was also a strange time of day for a drug transaction. Both the terrorists and the mafiosi had to have figured that all of the local lawmen had met someplace for lunch.

Bolan twisted the steering wheel and kicked up reddish-brown dust clouds beneath the Hummer's tires. He leaned onto the accelerator again, driving along the packed-dirt county road only slightly slower than he had on the pavement. His eyes searched the horizon ahead, and he saw Jessup lift a pair of binoculars.

"This ground isn't as flat as it looks," the DEA man said. "It looks like you ought to be able to see all the way to Canada. But you can't."

"We're only a few miles south of the Kansas state line and we can't even see that," the Executioner replied. "The terrain rises and falls so slowly and gently that it just looks flat. It can still block the view."

Jessup nodded and dropped the binoculars to his lap. Bolan drove on.

Two and a half miles later, the Hummer topped one of the gentle rises the Executioner had mentioned and suddenly they could see a group of vehicles parked in the middle of a cow pasture. One Jeep and five pickups were parked in a circle roughly a half mile in front of them and a quarter mile or so off the road. Bolan hit the brakes and slowed to a speed that wouldn't draw so much attention.

After all, the bright yellow Hummer was enough.

"Don't you think we ought to hurry on in?" Jessup asked, turning toward the Executioner.

Bolan slowed even further and shook his head. "They've seen us," he said. "Right about now, they're all looking this way and speculating on who we are. Wealthy farmers with more money than good sense who bought a big yellow play toy? Or the law? The law would swoop in fast. But it wouldn't be fast enough to keep most of them from getting away across the prairie."

"Not to mention the fact that they're going to start shooting as soon as it's obvious the law is after them." Jessup paused for a low chuckle, deep in his chest. "At least I'm the law," he said. "I still haven't figured out exactly who or what you are."

The Executioner chuckled himself. All Jessup knew was that he had been assigned to work with Bolan—whom he knew as Matt Cooper—for a series of drug deals to which his snitch was privy. He had already seen Cooper bend conventional law so far as to break it. But it was always for a final good, and the end really did always justify the means.

"You're right about the shooting," Bolan finally said. "As soon as I turn this baby their way, it's going to start. So the longer I can stay on the county road, the more it'll appear that we're just headed for someplace past them." He paused and took in a breath. "That means I'm going to wait until we're right across from them and then cut a hard right their way."

"Short of bringing in air support, that's about as good a plan as I can think of," Jessup said. He leaned forward and slid an AR-15 from beneath the Hummer's passenger's seat. Pulling back the bolt of the semiautomatic version of the military's M-16, he chambered a round, all the time keeping the weapon below the windows of the vehicle.

The Executioner knew he would need both hands on the wheel for the breakneck turn he had planned in the next few seconds, so he left his 9 mm Heckler & Koch MP-5 submachine gun where it lay near his feet. Then, as soon as he was perpendicular to the cars parked out in the cow pasture, he whipped the Hummer their way.

The Hummer fishtailed slightly as it descended into a deep bar ditch. Then it straightened again as it climbed up the other side. The sturdy personnel vehicle punched through the barbed-wire fence between two wooden posts as if it were snapping a dry rubber band. The razor-sharp barbs on the strands dragged across the Hummer's sides, scratching deeply into the yellow paint job. A second later, they were creating another dust storm behind them. But this time, the clouds flying up through the air from the Hummer's tires included not only dirt but long blades of wild grass.

Bolan and Jessup had been right in their assessment of the drug dealers' reaction.

The shooting started immediately.

The Executioner heard several engines roar to life, and then the Jeep and two of the pickups fled from the oncoming Hummer. The loud, frightened mooing of several dozen cattle, who had gathered together deeper into the pasture, rose up between the other noises as the escaping vehicles headed toward them, forcing the animals to part, and causing them to stampede in opposite directions.

The men escaping, Bolan knew, had to be the sellers, who already had their money. The buyers of the cocaine were still loading cardboard boxes into the backs of their vehicles from piles on the ground. But now they were forced to postpone that task and turn toward Bolan and Jessup.

"We can go after the guys with the money," Bolan said. "Or we can get the guys with the dope right here." He paused for a second, then added, "But we may not be able to get them both."

"Let's go for the dope," Jessup said without hesitation. "At least we can keep it from getting onto the streets."

"You're right," Bolan agreed. Reaching inside his light jacket, he drew the sound-suppressed Beretta 93-R. In the corner of his eye, he saw Jessup kneel his right leg on the seat, then wrap the seat belt tightly around his calf. As Bolan extended the Beretta out the window with his left hand, Jessup leaned out with his entire torso.

Both men began firing simultaneously.

As the Hummer crested a short rise in the pasture, it went momentarily airborne. Both the Executioner and the DEA agent waited for it to settle on flatter ground, then pulled their respective triggers.

A trio of subsonic, nearly inaudible 9 mm hollowpoint rounds rocketed from Bolan's Beretta. One round struck the shoulder of a man wearing a charcoal-gray suit and striped tie. Bolan frowned slightly, then nodded. The pickups the Mafia gunners had chosen fit right in with the landscape, but their clothing made them stand out.

Next to him, the Executioner heard Jessup pop off three semiauto rounds from his AR-15. They were still at least an eighth of a mile away, and none of the .223-caliber rounds seemed to find a target.

By now, the mafiosi in the field had taken cover around their pickups—three almost identical Toyota Tundras. One was burgundy colored, another green and the third one blue. All were parked with their beds facing the oncoming Hummer, the tailgates were down and the cargo areas roughly half-filled with cardboard boxes.

Cardboard boxes that, the Executioner knew, had to contain kilo after kilo of white powdered cocaine.

A rifle round struck the Hummer's windshield, then skimmed up off the bullet-resistant material. Only a tiny speck appeared on the glass to show where it had hit. Bolan drove on, squeezing the trigger of his Beretta yet again. This time all three rounds of automatic fire struck the right front fender of the green pickup as the same man he'd hit in the shoulder a little earlier ducked back behind the engine block.

Jessup fired again, and Bolan saw the rear windshield of the blue pickup shatter into thousands of tiny pieces.

"Dammit!" the DEA man shouted as he pulled his rifle back inside the Hummer.

Bolan glanced his way as he sped on toward the pickups. The still-smoking brass case from the last shot Jessup had fired stood straight up out of the breech of the weapon. Such a jam was called a stove pipe and it could come from a faulty magazine, a faulty round or a faulty gun.

Jamming the stock of his AR-15 back against the car seat, Jessup pulled back the bolt and brushed brass out of the weapon with a sweep of his left hand. His eyes stared down into the opening, and when he released the bolt again a fresh round was shoved into the chamber.

"I'm going to drive right through them," the Executioner said just as Jessup began to lean out of the window again. "This Hummer's the best cover we're going to get." His eyes narrowed as the brows above them furrowed. "And we may take out some of them in the crash." He paused for another quick glance over at Jessup. "Better stay in here and put your seat belt on right."

The DEA special agent understood. Taking a sitting position, he snapped his seat belt and shoulder harness into place, then rested his AR-15 across his lap with the barrel pointing at the door.

The mafiosi behind the pickups didn't realize what was going to happen until it was almost too late. They continued firing toward the Hummer, their rounds doing little more than make more specks on the windshield.

Then, suddenly, the fact that the huge civilianized military vehicle wasn't going to stop or even slow suddenly sank into them all at the same time. Six men suddenly emerged from behind the pickups and began running in different directions across the cow pasture.

The Hummer crashed into the tailgates of the burgundy and green Tundras, folded them up into a mangled mass of steel, then blew out all four of the rear tires. The burgundy truck was thrown out and to the left, directly atop one of the fleeing mafiosi.

The man's lone scream abruptly cut short as he was crushed to death. As soon as they were past the vehicles, the Executioner twisted the Hummer around in a breakneck U-turn and started back toward the crumpled green pickup. It had been knocked onto its side, and one of the mafiosi dived back behind the cab, not seeing any other possible escape.

But the overturned green pickup was no cover for the Hummer, either. Bolan turned the wheel slightly and a second later he and Jessup bumped up and over the wreck, squashing the Mafia soldier below their wheels and what remained of the green Toyota Tundra.

There had been a total of six men—two to a pickup.

The Hummer had taken care of two of them.

Now it was time to pursue the other four running in opposite directions across the wide-open spaces of the pastureland.

Bolan whipped the wheel to the right and accelerated once more. The Hummer dived and jumped over the uneven surface beneath its tires. Ahead, Bolan could see two of the running mafiosi—one wearing a charcoal-gray business suit, the other dressed in a more comfortable track suit—running as best they could. But regardless of the fact that he wore running clothes, the man inside them wasn't a runner. He was at least fifty pounds overweight and doing more waddling than actual running.

As they closed the gap to roughly ten yards, the fat man pulled a bright nickel-plated revolver from somewhere inside his jacket and threw a wild shot back at the Hummer. Bolan pushed the pedal down harder, and a second later the big vehicle was rolling along right next to the man.

The overweight Mafia man was huffing and puffing like a freight train on its final run before being scrapped. And it looked to the Executioner as if it took all of his last strength to lift the brightly shining wheelgun in his hand toward the open window of the Hummer.

Bolan extended his left hand out the window and tapped the trigger yet again.

All three 9 mm hollowpoint rounds coughed out of the sound-suppressed weapon and into the face and throat of the fat man.

Bolan drew a bead on the other man heading in the direction of the highway. He was on the other side of the Hummer, and Bolan said, "Get ready."

Jessup nodded and extended his rifle barrel out the window. But for this shot there would be no need to kneel on the seat or strap himself in. He could do it from where he sat.

A lone, frightened and confused cow suddenly appeared in front of them as if out of nowhere. The Executioner twisted the wheel hard, barely brushing past her without hurting her. The mooing sounded more like a roar as they drove on.

Fifteen seconds later, they were next to the man in the charcoal-gray suit. It was the same man Bolan had hit in the shoulder, and he held that shoulder with his other hand as he ran, a grimace of severe pain covering his face. But that hand also held a sawed-off 12-gauge shotgun, and as the Hummer neared, he attempted to raise it just as his overweight friend had tried with his nickel-plated revolver.

Jessup changed his plans. For life.

The Executioner watched out of the corner of his eye as the DEA agent lifted the barrel of his rifle and carefully triggered a double-tap of 5.56 mm NATO rounds into the mafioso. The first one caught the man in the center of the back, causing him to suddenly halt his running. The second round exploded the back of his head as he fell, leaving no question in either the Executioner's or Jessup's mind that he was dead.

Bolan wasted no time.

Another quick U-turn and the Executioner was already flooring the accelerator across the pasture. Ahead, he could see two tiny moving specks that he knew were the final two Mafia soldiers. They were still moving, but they looked as if they were tired. One speck had even slowed to a walk.

Bolan glanced to his right as they passed the wreckage of the other two pickups again. Far in the distance, hustling deeper into the pasture, he could see the Jeep and two pickups that had darted away as soon as the Hummer had left the road. If he and Jessup could just take out these last two mafiosi quickly enough, there was still the chance that they'd have time to catch up to the men escaping with the drug money.

Rolling on across the prairie, Bolan drove up next to the walking man. Dressed like the others, he had taken time to light a cigarette and now huffed and puffed on the unfiltered smoke that was clenched between his teeth.

As the Hummer neared, the man turned and looked back at it.

Bolan wondered if he might be able to take this man alive. If he could, he would. Not out of any sympathy for such a parasite who fed off the misery of others' addictions, but in order to collect information.

The Mafia man gave him no such chance.

As they neared the man, he turned and raised a small Skorpion submachine pistol. A smattering of bullets hit the windshield but the small, low-velocity rounds barely even marked the windshield. As they drove on, however, nearing the man, his angle of fire changed.

A second before he had a shot at Bolan through the driver's window of the Hummer, the Executioner extended his hand once more and tapped another 3-round burst into the man's face. Not even his mother would have recognized him as he settled on the grassy ground of the cow pasture.

Kicking their speed yet another notch, the Executioner came to a man who looked to be much younger than the other mafioso. In his early twenties, Bolan guessed, he was definitely in better shape. But the uneven pastureland was no cinder track, and the ruts and holes—not to mention the mounds that often crumbled under the feet—were slowing him.

The Hummer was still twenty yards behind him when the younger man turned. Instead of a business or track suit, he wore khaki slacks, a blue blazer and a paisley tie around the collar of his white button-down shirt. He looked more like a young attorney than a Mafia soldier, the Executioner thought as he twisted the steering wheel, turning his side of the truck to face this last man, then skidding to a halt.

The young man reached under his left armpit with his right hand.

But that was as far as he got toward his weapon.

The final 3-round burst in the Beretta's 15-round magazine flew out of the barrel with three quiet burps. All three hit the center of the mafioso's chest and exploded his heart. He fell straight back away from the Hummer, dead before he hit the ground.

The Executioner turned immediately for the vehicles still escaping across the pasture. They were at least a mile away now, and they'd be hard to intercept. Maybe impossible. It depended on whether they were just fleeing haphazardly or if they'd had some backup plan for a situation such as this.

Bolan frowned. They looked as if they knew what they were doing. And his gut instinct was that this escape route was part of a well-thought-out backup plan.

As he took his foot off the brake pedal and returned it to the accelerator, Jessup said, "You think there's a chance of catching them?"

The Hummer tore up more wild grass as it picked up speed. "I don't know," the Executioner said. "But it won't hurt to give it a shot."

BEHIND THE WHEEL of the Jeep, Harry Drake looked up into the rearview mirror. "Those bastards in that Hummer are coming after us," he told Sal Whitlow, who sat in the passenger's seat of the vehicle. Like Drake himself, Whitlow wore green camouflage BDUs and a boonie hat. A Russian Tokarev automatic pistol rode in a holster on his belt, and a Russian Kalashnikov AK-47 lay across his lap.

"They'll never catch us." Whitlow chuckled, turning in his seat to smile back into the pasture. "That yellow submarine's almost like a tank. But this Jeep and the four-wheel-drive pickups are enough for this terrain."

"I hope you're right," Drake said as he turned slightly to miss a small scrub tree. "And I hope our ticket out of here is waiting where he's supposed to be."

"He will be," Whitlow said confidently, turning back to face the front. "Joe Knox is solid SAS. I met him several times when we trained with the Brits."

Drake nodded. He was trusting Whitlow's judgment, as well as his word. They'd served together as Army Rangers during the first Gulf War, then worn the green beanies of the Army's Special Forces in both Afghanistan and Iraq. The two men were more than friends. They were like brothers.

Just the same, Drake was glad he'd downed a Lortab and a Xanax—painkillers—with a mouthful of whiskey right before the yellow Hummer appeared. His nerves had been on edge lately, and the mixture of drugs was sometimes all that kept him from screaming out loud.

As the Jeep took a rise, then suddenly plunged downward toward a dry creek bed, Drake twisted his neck and looked at the Ford F250. It was negotiating the rugged ground as well as the Jeep. He turned his head back and saw the Dodge Ram just outside his open-topped vehicle to his right. It was doing fine, too.

Whitlow was right. They had stolen the four-wheel-drive pickups, along with the Jeep, earlier that morning from a farm twenty miles away, and they'd been perfect vehicles in which to deliver the cocaine. And the farmer who had owned all three vehicles wouldn't need them anymore, either.

He and his wife lay dead on a pile of hay in the barn.

Drake took another quick glance at the Dodge Ram and saw Felix Bundy riding shotgun. Though he couldn't see past

Bundy in the higher vehicle, he knew Donald O'Hara was in the driver's seat. Both men had been Navy SEALS and served in the Middle East just like Drake and Whitlow. Drake glanced one more time at the Ford F250 as all three vehicles came up out of the creek bed and raced on toward a county section road just past a barbed-wire fence another two hundred yards away. Elmer Scott was behind the wheel of the Ram, with Charlie Ducket riding shotgun for him. The two of them had been U.S. Marine recons and had shot their share of Arabs just like the rest of the team.

Harry Drake instinctively ducked lower behind the Jeep's windshield as the front bumper burst through the barbed wire. The pickups had fallen in directly behind him, and now he raced up the bar ditch to the dirt road.

Drake frowned, thinking at lightning speed. The county road was a temptation. It would be easier going, with less chance of one or more of his convoy breaking down. But the Hummer would likely catch up to them more quickly if they took the easy route. Besides, once they reached the highway they'd be sitting ducks for Oklahoma highway patrolmen and any small-town cops who got word of what was going on over the radio.

By the time he had decided to go on through the next pasture he was already halfway down the bar ditch anyway. The Jeep popped the barbed wire surrounding the next quarter section as easily as it had the first one, and sent a small herd of Black Angus cattle scurrying away in terror.

As they raced across the pasture, Drake saw the white paint of the helicopter peeking between the branches of a small grove of trees. Behind the controls, he knew Joe Knox would be waiting to take them skyward. He slowed the Jeep and prepared to jump out, abandon it and help the men with the money load the briefcases before they abandoned the pickups.

As soon as he'd ground to a halt, Drake held his hand up to his eyes. Looking out over the pastureland, he could see the yellow Hummer just now crossing the county road and coming up through the hole in the fence that they had made.

"Okay, guys!" Drake yelled above the sound of the whopping chopper blades. "Get that money on board and let's get out of here!" He slung his AK-47 over his shoulder on the green web sling and hurried to the F250, where he seized four briefcases. "And from now until we're safely airborne, we change languages just in case!" A grin curled the corners of his mouth, making the ends of his handlebar mustache rise to tickle the sides of his nose.

He had chosen his crew carefully, including in his criteria for recruitment their exceptional combat skills, intelligence, willingness to break the laws of the nation that had trained them and they had defended, but even more for one other skill they all possessed.

Each and every one of Harry Drake's men spoke fluent Farsi, the national tongue of Iran.

"Aye-aye," one of the Marines yelled. Drake couldn't tell which one.

But it didn't matter. What did matter was that they get the half-million dollars in cash on board the chopper and fly out of here before that big yellow monstrosity of a vehicle arrived and its passengers shot them all.

Drake had a bad feeling about that canary-colored Hummer. Not so much the vehicle itself but the men inside it.

Something told him that at least one of the men—the driver, who had shown such competency in taking out their Mafia associates—was a superior warrior to each and every last one of them.

THE MAN DEA SPECIAL AGENT Rick Jessup had been told to call Matt Cooper continued to guide the yellow Hummer as it bounced in and out of the ruts and mounds that made up the cow pasture. Far in the distance, the specks that Jessup knew were a Jeep and two more pickups were gradually growing larger. As they banked down into another creek bed, then up the other side, he was suddenly able to differentiate between the vehicles. The Jeep was a standard CJ-5 model. One of the pickups was a Dodge Ram, the other a Ford F250.

Jessup couldn't remember the license numbers he had seen for a brief second as the three vehicles had fled the scene a few minutes earlier. But if memory served him right, they had all had local farm tags.

Which meant the men driving and riding in them had stolen them from somewhere close to this area. And they had to have stolen them recently. No reports of missing vehicles had gone out over the police-band radio mounted in the Hummer. That could only mean one of two things: either the rightful owners hadn't discovered their property missing yet or they were dead.

Considering the fact that his snitch had told him it was radical Islamic terrorists who had sold the coke to the Mafia, Jessup's money was on the latter possibility.

The DEA man watched the vehicles ahead of them slow, then stop as they reached a lone grove of trees in the middle of the pasture. Just above the treetops, he could barely make out the whirling blades of a helicopter.

"So that's their plan," Bolan said from behind the wheel. The words came out sounding hard and stark after the silence that had reigned over the Hummer for the past several minutes.

"They'll just abandon the pickups and Jeep. My guess is they were stolen anyway," Jessup said.

Bolan nodded, then turned briefly toward Jessup. "Take the wheel," he said.

Jessup reached over and grasped the steering wheel.

The Hummer slowed momentarily as Bolan took his foot off the accelerator and thrust himself backward over the seat into the rear passenger area of the Hummer. But it was done so quickly and smoothly—obviously a much-practiced move— that Jessup was able to slide behind the wheel and take control immediately.

A second later, Bolan had climbed back into the front, now in the passenger's seat where Jessup had been a second before. Reaching down to the floorboard, the big man lifted his Heckler & Koch MP-5 submachine gun.

Jessup got the Hummer back up to speed as Bolan strapped

his leg down with the seat belt. A moment later, he was more out of the window than in, and firing 3-round bursts from the H&K subgun.

Through the windshield, Jessup could see tiny figures loading what looked like briefcases from the pickups onto the helicopter. He also saw the small grass and dust storms erupt as his partner's 9 mm slugs fell a few feet in front of the men.

Out of the corner of his eye, Jessup watched Bolan raise his point of aim slightly. As more subgun explosions sounded from the other side of the Hummer, he looked out of the windshield again and saw two holes appear in the side of the chopper.

But they were still too far away for the submachine gun to be relied on for accuracy. It was a short-range weapon, and trying to force it to become a sniper's rifle was like using a screwdriver for a hammer.

Bolan tossed the MP-5 over his shoulder into the backseat and lifted the AR-15 that Jessup had used only minutes before on the Mafia men. He leaned out of the window again, and Jessup could see that the assault rifle was angled more horizontally this time. The 5.56 mm NATO rounds should reach the chopper more efficiently.

Bolan pulled the AR-15's trigger three times in a row, and a trio of rounds sailed across the grassland and pocked the side of the helicopter—just to the side of the open side door. But they did so as the last of the briefcases was loaded, and the last man in cammies reached up, took the hand of another terrorist and allowed himself to be jerked up into the chopper as it began to rise.

Bolan pulled the trigger several more times as the Hummer raced closer. But they were still too far away for his rounds to be effective, and to complicate things further, his target was moving as well as distant.

Jessup drove on. When the helicopter was perhaps a hundred feet in the air, the pilot turned its nose directly at the oncoming Hummer. Jessup watched as a man in green camouflage, secured to the helicopter by a ballistic nylon strap, leaned out of the same sliding side door through which the men had boarded.

Resting on his shoulder was an OD-green bazooka.

"Twist the wheel!" Bolan yelled. And even as he spoke, he dropped the AR-15 and reached across the Hummer with both hands.

The bazooka's charge exploded out of the mammoth barrel even as the back blast flew past the rear of the helicopter. Together, Bolan and Jessup turned the wheel as if their very lives depended on it.

The explosion ten feet to one side of their vehicle created a crater in the prairie ground roughly the same size that a hand grenade buried beneath the surface would have made. Bolan looked back up at the sky and saw the man with the bazooka disappear back into the helicopter. Then the chopper rose higher into the air, turned and flew away.

Jessup turned the Hummer back toward the helicopter as it grew smaller in the distance. Both he and Bolan stepped out of the yellow vehicle and watched.

"Any idea where they might be going?" Jessup asked.

Bolan shook his head. "Even on ground this flat, they'll be completely out of sight in another minute or so. Especially if they stay as close to the ground as they were. They could keep going, turn right or left, or even fly a few miles one way or another and then double back past us."

"They might figure we'll wait here and see," Jessup suggested.

"They might," Bolan said. "But it's not likely. They can spot this yellow Hummer a long time before we see them in the air. Come on." He got back behind the wheel of the big vehicle as Jessup jumped into the passenger's side. They drove only slightly slower as they returned to where the three Toyota pickups lay in ruins.

"It's gonna take a while to get all that coke rounded up, inventoried and loaded," Jessup said as they neared the overturned truck. "Want me to radio in for some assistance?" He started to reach for the microphone mounted on the dashboard.

Bolan shook his head and Jessup's arm froze in midair.

"I've got a faster and much more efficient way of handling

things," the big man said as he pulled up next to the overturned truck. Quickly dropping down from the Hummer, the Executioner walked to the back of the Hummer and grabbed a five-gallon can of gasoline. Then, walking from truck to truck, he dribbled a trail of gas in his wake, removing the cap to each pickup's gas tank when he reached it.

Finally, Bolan dripped gas in his tracks as he walked backward to the Hummer once more. Punching the cigarette lighter into the dash, he turned to Jessup as the DEA man got in on the other side. "You don't smoke, do you?" he asked.

"No," Jessup said.

Bolan nodded. Pulling the cigarette lighter out of the Hummer's dash, he glanced for a second at the glowing orange disk inside it, then dropped it out of the window.

The gasoline-soaked prairie grass next to the Hummer immediately started to burn, and the flame worked its way down the individual trails that led to the Toyotas, cocaine and dead men.

Throwing the Hummer into gear, Bolan tore up more grass and dirt as he floored the accelerator and raced back to the county road. He had driven through broken barbed-wire fence and traversed the bar ditch to the road when the explosions began.

2

Bolan watched the flames leaping in the rearview mirror as he drove the Hummer back toward the highway. Next to him, Jessup had turned sideways in his seat and watched as the three exploded pickups, the dead mafiosi and a half-million dollars of cocaine burned. "Well, Cooper," he said finally, turning back to face the front. "That's certainly a lot easier than bagging it all for evidence and transporting it for safekeeping until the trial—which won't be necessary now anyway." He paused and took a deep breath. "You *sure* we aren't going to have to answer for this? I mean, calling this unorthodox behavior for a law-enforcement officer would be the understatement of the century."

"Don't sweat it, Jessup," Bolan said. "Yes, I'm in charge of this operation. But I'm not a law-enforcement officer."

The DEA man threw his head back against the neck rest atop his seat. "Oh, that's great," he said. "So you're a spook. CIA? Department of Defense? Homeland Security?"

"Uh-uh," the Executioner said. Ahead, he could see where the dirt rose up to the two-lane highway leading from Guyman to Boise City. "None of those."

"Okay," Jessup said. "I'll quit wondering exactly who you are or who you work for. It doesn't matter. You're one hell of a…" He stopped talking for a second, looking for the right words. When he didn't find them, he continued, "You're one damn fine fighter. You immediately adapt to whatever situation presents itself." Across the front seat, the Executioner saw him frown. "But do you not have to answer to anyone? Anyone at all?"

"Just the President," Bolan said. "And we get along just fine."

He withdrew his scrambled satellite phone and tapped in a number. A few seconds later, Jack Grimaldi answered the summons.

"Yeah, Striker," the ace pilot acknowledged. "What's up?"

"We got the dope but missed the money," Bolan told him. "We're headed back to Guyman now to meet you."

"You can do that if you want," Grimaldi said, "but there's no need to. I took a little recon flight an hour or so ago. Spotted your bright yellow vehicle on the road. But the important thing here is the terrain I saw. It's so flat, I'd have to try hard to find a place where I *couldn't* land." He stopped speaking for a second so Bolan could take it all in, then said, "Want me to come to you? It'll be a lot faster."

"Sounds fine," the Executioner said. He pulled off the highway onto the shoulder and threw the Hummer into Park. The entire roadway was asphalt, pocked with holes the size of volcanoes and, in general, rougher riding than the cow pastures had been. Pulling a small handheld Global Positioning Unit—GPU—out of his shirt pocket, he read the Hummer's coordinates to Grimaldi. "When you start smelling smoke and seeing flames below, you'll know you're close."

"That's affirmative, big guy," Grimaldi said. "I'm revving her up now. See you in a few."

Bolan heard a click in his ear and folded his phone back before dropping it and the GPU into his pockets again. Then he leaned back in his seat and closed his eyes. "You never know when we'll get another chance to rest once this mission gets off the ground," he told Jessup. "So I'd suggest you take advantage of it now."

IT SEEMED THAT BOLAN had just closed his eyes when he was awakened by the distinctive sound of twin Pratt & Whitney PW305 turbofan engines. He turned to Jessup, grabbed the DEA agent's arm and gently shook him to consciousness.

Bolan smiled when the pilot landed and brought the Learjet 60 to a halt less than twenty yards away. His friend controlled whatever craft he was flying as if it were an extension of his body. Aircraft were to Grimaldi what firearms and other weapons were to the Executioner.

When Jessup was awake, both men got out of the Hummer, walked down and then up across the bar ditch, then climbed over the fence. The Executioner found the door to the Learjet already open when he reached it, and Jack Grimaldi grinning at him below his sunglasses.

A second later, Bolan had strapped himself into his seat next to the pilot and Jessup took the seat behind Grimaldi. The ace pilot revved the engines, and the plane began to pick up speed again in preparation for takeoff.

The Executioner withdrew his sat phone and tapped in the number to Stony Man Farm, America's top-secret counterterrorist headquarters. Bolan maintained an arm's-length working relationship with Stony Man, and his and the Farm's missions often coincided.

Barbara Price, Stony Man Farm's mission controller, didn't answer until the fourth ring. "Sorry, Striker," she said. "I was busy transferring some data to Bear."

Aaron "the Bear" Kurtzman was in charge of the banks of computers and personnel who gathered the Farm's electronic intel. Kurtzman spent most of his life in front of a computer. Once a strong bear of a man, he had been paralyzed from the waist down during a gun battle years ago and was now confined to a wheelchair.

And he was the best. There were simply no programs into which he couldn't hack if given enough time, and there was no computer that came close to the power of his own brain. He had proved invaluable to Bolan and the other teams that worked out of the Farm.

"So what's new on the western front?" Price said.

"We got the Mafia scum and the coke," Bolan told the honey-blond mission controller. "Just missed the sellers."

"Did you hear any of them speak?" Price asked.

Under normal conditions, the question would have sounded straight out of left field. But Bolan knew why Price had asked him. "Uh-uh," he said. "We never got close enough to hear voices. They spoke to us with bullets and a bazooka."

"A bazooka?" Price said.

"That's right," the Executioner said. "They missed."

"Obviously," Price said. "You need to talk to Hal?"

"Yeah," the Executioner said. "Put him on."

Bolan heard a click in his ear as Price put him on hold and went about her search for Hal Brognola, the Farm's director. But he was also a high-ranking official within the U.S. Department of Justice. High enough, at least, that no one questioned his frequent and unexplained absences from Washington, D.C., during which time he manned the reins of Stony Man. He was also Bolan's link to conventional law enforcement, and could get most things done with a simple phone call.

The Learjet continued to gain altitude, then leveled off as Bolan waited. A few minutes later, he heard the voice of another old friend.

"What's happening, big guy?" Hal Brognola said into the phone.

"Just finished with the coke deal. Killed the bad guys, exploded the dope. There may be a few hundred cattle who get wired if the wind blows in the right direction, but that should be the only damage."

Brognola laughed. "Better them than humans," he said. "Barb already told me. Sounds like you came close to catching the pushers, too."

"Yeah. Too bad we weren't playing horseshoes."

"Any idea who they were?" Brognola questioned. "Any chance they were this Islamic terrorist group that's been robbing banks and creating other forms of havoc all over the place?"

"Hard to say, Hal," the Executioner replied. "We didn't get close enough to really get a good look at them. And as I suspect Barbara already told you, we couldn't hear them speaking."

"So tell me what your hunches are, big guy," Brognola said. "They usually turn out to be as accurate as anything that can be proved."

"My guess is that they're the same bunch that hit the bank in Kansas City yesterday. They drove two pickups and a Jeep to the scene but had a helicopter waiting for them to make their getaway. I'd guess the chopper is theirs, which makes the Oklahoma panhandle only a hop, skip and a jump from K.C. The other vehicles I suspect they stole locally. And recently. There haven't been any such theft reports come out over the police-band radio."

"Anything else?" Brognola asked.

"Just that they were well trained. Either in one of the Middle-Eastern terrorist-training camps or some country's armed forces. They worked with a certain military precision that I can't quite put my finger on. And one more thing."

"What's that?"

"The guy who fired the bazooka at us—there was something about him I can't put my finger on. But my gut tells me he's no more Arabic than you or me."

"Why's that?" Brognola asked.

"I can't say for sure. Maybe something about the way he moved. I really don't know."

"You sound like you're leaning away from the radical-Islamic-terrorist theory," Brognola said.

"Not entirely. But I'm certainly questioning it."

"When you think about it, these guys have done a lot of things to make it look like their crimes were for religious and political reasons," Brognola said. "Almost gone out of their way to convince people of it."

"That's what I'm beginning to think," the Executioner said. "Stop and think about it, Hal. There've been three kidnappings and a little over a half-dozen bank robberies attributed to these men. The only witness left alive was that pregnant woman yesterday. She said they spoke Arabic. But do you think she could tell Arabic from one of the other Middle-Eastern languages? Like Farsi, maybe?"

"I doubt it," Brognola said. "In fact, I'm not sure half of my own agents could."

"Right," the Executioner said. "I'm not saying they aren't radical Muslims of some sort. Just that we can't be sure yet."

"So what can I do for you at this point?" Brognola asked.

Bolan glanced to Jessup in the backseat. The DEA man was sitting forward again, straining to hear every word that Bolan said. Turning his attention back to the phone once more, the Executioner said, "I'd like you to pull whatever strings you have to in order to get Jessup assigned to me for the duration of this mission. Think you can pull that off?"

"All it'll take is a phone call," Brognola said. "What have you got planned next?"

Bolan glanced behind him, toward the Learjet's storage area. He had come straight to this mission from another strike in Australia, and was running low on ammo and other equipment. It was definitely time to restock.

"I'm coming in," the Executioner told Brognola. "We're running short on supplies."

There was a long pause on the other end of the line. Then Brognola said, "You still have Jessup with you, right?"

Bolan knew what the pause had meant. Stony Man Farm was a top-secret installation. From the road, it looked like a regular working farm in the Shenendoah Valley. Knowledge of its location, as well as its function, was strictly on a need-to-know basis. And Jessup didn't need to know.

"I've got him but I'll take care of it," the Executioner said. "Talk to you later." He hung up.

Reaching under the seat next to Grimaldi, the Executioner pulled out what looked like a black cotton sack. But a small hole right in the middle would have raised the eyebrows of anyone seeing the bag for the first time.

Bolan turned around to Jessup. "I'm sorry to have to do this, Jessup," he said. "But it's necessary that you ride the rest of the way to my base of operations wearing this."

Rick Jessup just shrugged. Then, taking the hood from

Bolan, he pulled it down over his head and positioned the hole over his nose so he could breathe.

Then Jessup settled back in his seat, and Bolan turned back and did the same.

AS SOON AS HE'D PUNCHED the proper code buttons on the panel next to the steel door, Bolan heard the buzzer and pushed the door open. The Executioner held the door for Jessup, ushering the still-hooded man inside. He then loosened the cord around Jessup's neck and removed the hood.

Hal Brognola was already seated at the head of the long conference table in Stony Man Farm's War Room. A manila file was open in front of the Justice man on the table, and the stub of an unlit cigar was clenched between his teeth.

Seated to the Stony Man director's left was a distinguished-looking man wearing a navy-blue business suit. Although obviously older, he had a full head of medium-length white hair and a short beard and mustache of the same snowy hue.

Bolan had never seen him before in his life.

"Come in, come in," Brognola said, looking up briefly from the papers in his file. "Take a seat, both of you."

The Executioner dropped down onto the padded chair to Brognola's right. Jessup blinked his eyes rapidly, trying to adjust to the new light, as he took the seat next to Bolan. He continued to squint as Brognola looked up, frowning slightly at Bolan.

"Where's Jack?" the big Fed asked.

"I put him in charge of overseeing the Lear's restocking," Bolan answered.

"You can fill him in while you're in the air," Brognola said.

Brognola glanced at the man with the white beard and hair. "First, I'd like to introduce Mr. John Sampson."

Sampson leaned across the table and shook hands with both Bolan and Jessup. Bolan introduced himself as Matt Cooper. Jessup used his real name.

Brognola spoke again. "Mr. Sampson's reason for being here, and his role in this mission, will become apparent as we go." He looked back down at the open file in front of him and said, "So far, this group we're interested in has been responsible for seven bank robberies in the Midwest, three kidnappings— with two of the victims found dead even though the ransom was paid—and they appear to have a Mexican connection for both cocaine and heroin. That deal you just broke up, it was—"

"I wouldn't say we broke it up," the Executioner interrupted. "The guys with the money got away."

"At least the dope won't hit the street," Brognola said, using almost the identical words Jessup had chosen back in the Oklahoma panhandle. He cleared his throat and then continued. "The third kidnap victim is the daughter of a Georgia state senator," he said. "The FBI's negotiating her release even as we speak."

"A release that won't happen until she's dead," Bolan said.

"That's what the two earlier kidnappings would suggest," Brognola came back.

"How much are they demanding, Hal?" Bolan asked.

"An even million."

Jessup let out a high-pitched whistle.

"Are we sure that all these crimes—the drug deals, robberies, kidnaps—can be attributed to the same group of men?" Bolan said.

"Reasonably sure," Brognola said. "In all of the bank jobs they wore Nam leaf cammies and black ski masks. There's enough similarities in their method of operation inside the banks to tip the scales that way, too. Some variance in height and weight descriptions, skin color on their hands and such. But that's to be expected."

The Executioner nodded. He knew that if a hundred people watched the same crime go down, you'd get a hundred different versions of the story. The human mind played tricks on the average citizen who encountered the unusual life-or-death situation, and investigating officers had to take such things into account.

"The primary link, though, is that everyone at the banks— and I mean *everyone*—agreed that they spoke a foreign language when communicating with each other. Most thought it was Arabic but weren't sure."

"Arab terrorists are always the first to come to mind these days," Bolan noted. "It doesn't mean that they *aren't* Arabs. But it doesn't mean that they *are,* either."

All of the heads around the table nodded their agreement. Then Brognola said, "And when they shouted out orders to the customers, it was in broken English and heavily accented."

"Broken English is easy enough to fake, too," Bolan said. "Not that I'm discounting the possibility that they're Arabs of some kind. Just playing the devil's advocate here."

"I know," Brognola said, nodding.

"What about the negotiations on the kidnappings?" Jessup asked.

"Same thing," Brognola said. "All done in broken English, with a heavy accent of some kind. There's another kind of strange aspect to these abductions, though," he added.

"And it is?" the Executioner said.

"They haven't warned the parents about going to the police. Fact is, they've ordered them to. Told them they wouldn't negotiate any ransom or releases with anyone except the FBI."

"That does sound a little off the wall," Jessup said.

"Maybe not," Bolan said, shaking his head. "These men—Arabs, Iranians or whoever they actually are—were trained someplace and trained well. So far, I'd put their skills right up there with our own Special Forces."

Brognola looked a little surprised. Bolan, he well knew, was former Army Special Forces himself, and now he was comparing these robbers, kidnappers and murderers to other men like himself.

Bolan directed a weary smile at his old friend. "Don't take that wrong, Hal," he said. "All I'm saying is that as well as being more-than-competent fighters, they're smart. And they know that while the FBI will be trying to catch them, the Feds won't pull anything stupid that puts the victim in further jeopardy. They'll ask for an FBI agent to deliver the money, too, is my guess. Because the Feds' first concern is getting the girl back safe and sound. Fathers—now, that's a different story. They aren't trained for situations like this, and holding up under this kind of pressure is just flat-out impossible for most men. The kidnappers know if they deal with a father or husband, or any other family member, they're dealing with a loose cannon. Their behavior is completely unpredictable while the FBI agent's isn't."

The room went silent for a few seconds, then Brognola turned toward the man with the white hair and beard. "Now, let me tell you exactly where Mr. John Sampson fits into all this."

"You want to cut out that 'Mr.' stuff, please?" Sampson said. "We're all in this together, and I don't see any of us wearing military uniforms anymore."

Brognola gave the man a weary smile. "John was 101st Airborne in Nam," he said. "Served two tours. Then he went to work in the oilfields of Iran for two years—that was back when the shah was still running the show—before coming back here and starting his own oil company. He sold the oil company a few years ago and became a professor at George Washington University."

"So what do you teach, John?" Jessup asked. "Geology or something?"

"Not even close," Sampson said. "Linguistics."

"John noticed some discrepancies in the way some of the bank robbers spoke," Brognola cut in. "He just happened to be one of the customers in one of the banks when it was robbed."

Sampson nodded. "What I did learn, and what I can tell you, is that they weren't Arabs. Or at least they weren't speaking Arabic. It was Farsi. Most definitely Farsi."

Bolan studied Sampson's penetrating stare. Finally, the man with the white beard sat back in his chair again. "And I can tell you another thing," Sampson said. "Farsi was a *second* language with them."

"How could you know that?" Jessup asked.

Bolan knew the answer, but he let Sampson explain it for Jessup's benefit.

"Because," Sampson said, "while they were fluent in the language, a lot of it was what I'd call textbook Farsi. Way too formal for actual speech. You know how people who learned English in a classroom instead of growing up with it talk? It was sort of like that."

"Iran and Iraq are next-door neighbors," Bolan said. "It's not that unusual for people from both countries—especially along the border—to speak both languages."

"You're right," Sampson said, turning back to the Executioner. "But these bank robbers all had really strange accents— the likes of which I never heard when I was living in that part of the world. And believe me, I traveled all over Iran. I *still* couldn't place their accents." He paused long enough to lean back in his seat and cross his arms. "And there's one other thing," he said.

Bolan, Jessup and Brognola waited for him to go on.

"When they spoke English, they had these phony-sounding Arabic accents."

Bolan continued to study the man with the white beard. He appeared to be in decent physical condition, and he was obviously intelligent and well-spoken. In both English and Farsi.

He might just become invaluable during the rest of this mission.

Looking back to Brognola, Bolan said, "When you put all of the facts together—bank robberies, kidnappings for ransom, drug deals—it all comes down to money. Whoever these guys are, they're trying to get together as much money as they can. And what do you do with money?" he asked.

"Buy things," Jessup said.

"Exactly." Bolan nodded. "But they're hitting so hard and so fast that they don't have any time to spend any of what they take in. To me, that means they're getting ready to purchase a specific item that is expensive. There's something out there that these guys want to buy, and they're working toward that goal."

"What do you think it is they want?" Jessup asked.

"I don't know," Bolan said. "At least not for sure yet. But I've got an idea."

"What's that?" Brognola asked.

"Hal," Bolan replied, "I'd rather not say quite yet because I could be wrong. And I don't want to unduly prejudice anyone else's ideas as we go about tracking down these guys."

Brognola just nodded.

The Executioner turned toward Sampson again. "What's your immediate future look like, John? Would you be able to take off a few days and work with us? It would sure help to have somebody who can speak Farsi."

Sampson smiled. "Did I mention that I also speak Arabic and Hebrew?"

Bolan chuckled. "No," he said. "But that's two more gold stars for taking you with us. And your military experience won't hurt, either. Can you swing it?"

Sampson smiled, showing a row of teeth every bit as white as his hair. "I'm a millionaire oilman," he said. "I can do anything I want."

"So, do you want to?" Bolan asked.

"Wouldn't miss it for the world," Sampson shot back. "Just give me some firepower and point me in the right direction."

"Then it's settled," Bolan said, looking back to Brognola again. "They should have the Lear almost loaded by now." He started to rise.

"Where are you going to start?" Brognola wanted to know.

"I'd say that the state senator's daughter in Georgia demands priority," Bolan answered. "Especially since the other two hostages were murdered."

Brognola nodded. "I'll call ahead to the FBI field office in Atlanta," he said. "Tell them to be expecting you."

THE LEARJET WAS WAITING, with Jack Grimaldi behind the controls, by the time Bolan and Brognola helped the hooded Jessup and Sampson up into the passenger area. The Executioner buckled himself in, then said over his shoulder, "Buckle up. You can take the hoods off about five minutes into our flight."

Grimaldi had been warming up the engine. But before he

could start his takeoff, a figure appeared through the window, running toward them. Bolan turned to watch as John "Cowboy" Kissinger continued to hurry toward them, finally coming to a halt next to the door beside Bolan.

The Executioner opened it.

Kissinger was Stony Man Farm's chief armorer, and a true master of weaponry and other equipment. He was constantly inventing, or improving, the equipment used by all of the counterterrorists who worked out of Stony Man.

Now, as soon as the door was open, he reached down into the front pocket of his faded blue jeans.

Bolan's eyes followed Kissinger's hand, and he watched as the armorer drew a pocket-clipped folding knife. "Check this out," he told the Executioner, extending the knife in his hand.

Bolan took the folder and looked down at it. It was long and lean, and thicker at the hilt than at the tapered pommel. A thumb-stud opener was screwed into the blade next to a slight, half-moon indentation in the grip. Bolan flicked the stud with his thumb, and the blade sprang open.

The dagger-shaped blade looked to be a shade over four inches in length. But it was ground on one side only. The Executioner read the inscriptions on both sides of the steel. Caledonian Edge, San Mai III, and on the other side, Cold Steel, Japan.

"Looks like a good piece," Bolan told Kissinger.

"Oh, it is, it is," the armorer replied. "I polished the rocker a little bit more, but it really didn't need much custom work. It's custom-made in Japan already. The blade shape comes from the old Scottish sock knives."

Bolan nodded and started to hand the knife back.

But Kissinger took a step away from him and shook his head. "Take it with you," he said. "Then tell me how it stands up in the field. I'm thinking about offering them to everyone here at the Farm who wants one."

"Will do," Bolan said. "Always happy to risk my life as your guinea pig for untested products." He was smiling when he spoke. The truth was, he had complete faith in Kissinger's judgment.

Kissinger waved goodbye as Bolan closed the door. The Learjet was warmed up now, and Grimaldi began to guide it down the runway. Bolan sat back in his seat. The flight to Georgia would not take long, especially in the Learjet. But what little time it took could still be put to good use.

Flipping open a panel on the armrest nearest the door, the Executioner pulled up a folding work table and spread it across his lap. Next, he placed the file Brognola had given him on the table and opened it.

The only intelligence information he was interested in at the moment was in regard to the kidnapped daughter of the state senator in Georgia, and he found all of the reports held together by a paper clip on top of the rest of the information about the robberies and other crimes.

Behind him, the Executioner could hear Sampson and Jessup whispering softly. Grimaldi, to his side, took the Lear down the runway and into the air. When they had reached flying altitude, Bolan began shuffling through the pages.

Sarah Ann Pilgrim, eighteen, daughter of Henry and Myra Pilgrim, had been abducted by several men when she'd left her seat in the bleachers of a high school baseball field to visit the ladies' room. Witnesses described her abductors as heavily armed with assault rifles and pistols, wearing green-and-brown Army clothes and black ski masks. The kidnappers had contacted Sarah's parents the next day, demanding an immediate payment of a million dollars or they'd never see their daughter alive again. Henry Pilgrim, being an honest politician, had cried over the phone that he would never be able to raise that much money.

His tears had bought him an extra day. Nothing else.

Knowing that he was out of his league in both the financial arena and in handling terrorists and professional criminals, Henry had called in the FBI. One of the Bureau's trained hostage negotiators was now in contact with whoever was on the other end of the phone calls, and doing his best to stall for more time. FBI technicians were also trying to trace the calls, but so far their attempts had been fruitless. The kidnappers were using a different cell phone each time they called, and evidently moving around Atlanta in some kind of vehicle. By the time the Bureau men could triangulate a call, they had moved to another area and were using a different phone.

The Executioner finished skimming the reports and closed the file. He closed his eyes, seeing the photograph that had been with the other paperwork now on the back of his eyelids. Sarah Ann Pilgrim was a cute little strawberry-blond girl who had all the earmarks of someday growing into a beautiful, mature woman. She was standing next to what looked like a ski boat of some kind in the picture, clad only in a bikini.

Bolan found his upper and lower teeth grinding against each other in silent anger. He could only pray that the kidnappers were nothing more than perpetrators of crimes for money. If there was a rapist among them—

The Executioner turned his thoughts away from such things. It would do no good to brood over the possibilities. He was already doing everything he could to locate and rescue Sarah Ann, and he would get her to safety as soon as possible.

The Executioner opened the file again and read through all of the reports, then found himself frowning. Shifting the reports regarding Sarah Ann's abduction to the right side of the table, he began shuffling through the pages that dealt with the robberies. The frown grew deeper as he read on, occasionally referring back to the reports concerning Sarah Ann Pilgrim and the other two victims who had been abducted—and murdered.

The time frames concerning some of these crimes simply didn't add up. If it was the same men perpetrating all of these crimes, they had kidnapped another girl in Boston, and fifteen minutes later robbed a bank in Wilmer, Minnesota.

Not even Jack Grimaldi could get you from Massachusetts to the southern Minnesota town of Wilmer that fast.

Other bank robberies had gone down during the periods that these camo-clad men had had their kidnap victims in custody and still alive. The parents of the girl from Boston, as well as those of a young man from Albuquerque, had spoken to their children.

So who was keeping an eye on them while the others went running around the country robbing banks? Now the furrows on Bolan's forehead deepened even further. There had to be at least two factions of this gang or terrorist cell using the same MO. Were they together in this, or separate? Together. They had to be.

The similarities were simply too many to be coincidence.

The Executioner closed the file again as Grimaldi spoke into his microphone, gaining clearance for their landing in Atlanta. The Learjet began its descent, and a few minutes later they were taxiing toward an aluminum-sided hangar reserved for private aircraft.

"Jack, you mind taking care of the paperwork?" the Executioner said as a dark black Chevrolet sedan made its way toward them. It had so many antennae extending up from the hood and trunk that it could only have been a police vehicle of some kind.

"No problem," Grimaldi said. "I'll stay here with the plane."

Bolan opened the cargo door and began removing black nylon cases that, in addition to clothes, held weapons, ammunition, extra magazines and other equipment. Bolan, Jessup and John Sampson lifted their luggage and walked to where the black sedan had parked next to the hangars. The door opened, and a man wearing an expensive suit, a white shirt and black sunglasses stepped out. He wore his black hair in a short flattop cut, and his hairline was just beginning to recede.

"You Cooper?" he asked Bolan in short, clipped syllables. It was obvious that he wasn't glad to be where he was, doing what he was doing, as he got out of the sedan and walked to the rear of the car, inserting a key into the trunk.

"I am," Bolan told him. He pointed to Jessup and started to say, "This is Rick—"

"Jessup," the FBI agent interrupted. "DEA. And the guy with the Santa Claus hair and beard must be the linguistics specialist your man at Justice told us about when he called down earlier."

By now the bags were in the trunk and the four men found

seats in the sedan. The FBI man took the wheel again, Bolan rode shotgun and Sampson and Jessup got into the back. "You haven't told us your name yet," Bolan said.

"I'm Special Agent Wilkerson, in charge of the Atlanta office," came the reply in the same clipped tone.

"Ah, the special agent in charge has come to greet us himself," Jessup said from the backseat.

Bolan felt his jaw tighten slightly. The competition between the DEA and FBI was legendary. He just hoped Jessup and Wilkerson didn't let it get out of hand.

If they did, the Executioner would have to come down on them both, hard and fast. Such rivalries did nothing but get in the way on a mission like this.

Before Wilkerson could reply, Jessup went on. "We're a pretty informal group, you'll find," he said.

Wilkerson threw the automobile into Drive and started toward an exit.

The DEA man continued talking. "What's your first name, Wilkerson?"

"Special," Wilkerson said with even more venom in his words than he'd already shown.

"Cute," Jessup said. "Very cute. So I suppose that would mean you've got three middle names? Agent, In and Charge?"

"That's right, DEA man," Wilkerson said.

"Mind if I ask you one more question?" Jessup said.

"Go right ahead."

"Who stuck the broom handle up your ass?" Jessup asked quietly and calmly.

Bolan had not entered into the conversation because, so far, his words hadn't been needed. But now it appeared that the anger Wilkerson was exhibiting went far and above the usual interagency squabbling. It was time to nip it in the bud.

By now, the sedan had left the airport, navigated a cloverleaf entrance ramp and was on the divided highway leading into Atlanta. But as soon as Wilkerson heard Jessup's remark about the broomstick, an angry snort shot from his nostrils. He twisted the Chevy's wheel hard to the right, pulling it over onto the shoulder of the highway before throwing it violently into Park.

Turning, he rested one arm on the back of the bench seat that both he and Bolan occupied. "Okay, you want to know why I'm pissed off?" he said. "I'll tell you. We—the Atlanta FBI office—already have everything under control. We don't need your help, and we particularly don't like having you guys thrust down our throats by whoever the bigwig friend of yours in Justice is. But you want to know the worst thing of all?" Now he looked directly at the Executioner. "It's being told we all—even me, the SAC—have to take orders from this Cooper character who none of us has ever met or even heard of."

Bolan surprised him by letting a friendly smile encompass his face, then saying, "I don't blame you. I'd be mad if I was in your shoes, too. But you don't have the whole picture of what's going on."

Wilkerson looked confused as his eyes locked with those of the Executioner. Bolan's was a response he hadn't counted on, and the look on Jessup's face told the Executioner that it wasn't the feedback he'd have gotten if the DEA man had had a chance to answer the accusation.

"And you have the whole picture?" Wilkerson asked in the semisurly voice Bolan had grown to expect out of the man.

"No," the Executioner said. "If we had the whole picture, all this would be over and the bad guys would be in jail or dead. But let me say—and I say this with all due respect to you and the rest of the Atlanta FBI—while we don't have all the pieces to this puzzle yet, we've got more than you guys do. So let's work together, okay?"

There was only a trace of anger left in his voice as Wilkerson pulled the black FBI sedan back onto the divided highway. Several minutes went by in silence as they made their way into the city. Then, suddenly, Wilkerson blurted out, "Greg."

Bolan turned in his seat. In the corner of his eye, he could see the two men in the backseat were as puzzled as he was. "What's that mean?" Bolan asked. "Greg who?"

"Greg," Wilkerson said again. "Short for Gregory. It's my first name." He glanced up into the rearview mirror and his face lifted in a genuine smile. "And I've only got one middle name, just like most people."

"What is it?" Jessup asked.

"Wild horses couldn't drag *that* out of me," Wilkerson said as the outskirts of Atlanta appeared in the distance.

"I think I like the first name you gave us earlier better," Jessup said. "Special. Has a nice ring to it."

The look on Wilkerson's face betrayed his confusion. "I'm not sure what you mean by that," he said.

"Tell you what," Jessup said. "Why don't you start off our newfound friendship by telling us where we're going, Special?"

Now, all of the rest of the warriors in the car got the joke and laughed.

3

They were headed to the Pilgrims' house.

Wilkerson knew the city and took an exit off the highway onto an asphalt road that led through a rural area within the city limits. Bolan noted that every few miles the site-prep work for houses or apartments or office buildings had begun. Some plots already had the wooden forms where the concrete would be poured. Others already had their foundations in place, and some of the framing was beginning to go up.

Ten miles after turning off the highway, Wilkerson pulled up to a closed iron gate. A uniformed man stood in the guard shack, but when he recognized Wilkerson he pushed the button to open the iron. As the gate swung slowly back, Bolan looked past it to a sign implanted in the lush green grass. EasyRest Estates, it read.

Beyond the gate Wilkerson took a right-hand turn and then a left, looping back. The houses they passed were all made of rough-hewn stone, and Bolan doubted that any of them could be had for less than a half-million in the slumping housing market.

Several vehicles resembling their own sedan were parked along the street and in a driveway just ahead. Bolan also saw a van he guessed to be not only a storage area for body armor, weapons and other gear but also a rolling communications and surveillance vehicle. His suspicions were confirmed as they passed the white van and he saw the tiny nub of a periscope barely sticking out of the top.

Wilkerson had to park two houses down, in front of a neighbor's house. As the four men walked toward the door,

Jessup said, "Hey, Special. I thought you said Pilgrim wasn't rich. This development doesn't exactly look like a soup line for the homeless."

Wilkerson laughed. He had become used to Jessup's teasing now. "Don't let the house fool you," the FBI man said as they crossed the lawns to the Pilgrims' front porch. "Henry Pilgrim's wife inherited this place from her parents when they died. And everything else Pilgrim's got—which doesn't even come close to a million dollars—is tied up in stocks, bonds and CDs." He reached the front porch and led the way up the steps. "They've got a little over two thousand bucks in a couple of checking accounts, and around ten grand in savings."

"You checked them out?" John Sampson asked as he, Bolan and Jessup followed the FBI man up the steps to the porch.

Wilkerson didn't turn. "Standard procedure," he said. "Checked the credit union, too. They're clean. Not even behind on a car payment."

Bolan nodded. It was standard procedure. More than once, people who were deeply in debt instigated their own fake kidnappings, hoping that monetary donations would be sent to them by a sympathetic public. This didn't appear to be one of those times.

The Executioner could hear the din and chatter inside the house before Wilkerson even opened the door. Bolan let the FBI agent hold the door for Jessup and Sampson, then took it from him and let him duck under his arm before being the last to enter the house.

The living room looked more like a NASA command center during a space-shuttle fight than it did the plush, exquisitely furnished and decorated living room Bolan knew it had to have been the day before. Agents from the Atlanta office had run a half-dozen phone lines through the front windows into the house. Though each and every agent in the room had a cell phone, if too many of them started making calls at the same time, their transmissions and receptions would turn to total bedlam.

Only one man was actually using a phone at the moment. He sat in a puffed reclining armchair, leaning forward with a gold receiver pressed against his ear. When he saw Wilkerson walk in he ended the conversation quickly.

The room went quiet, and for the first time Bolan noticed the man and woman who sat holding hands on a love seat next to the front picture window. The woman's eyes were red and swollen, and she held a crumpled tissue to her nose. Other wadded and discarded balls of tissue had begun to pile up at her feet.

Bolan looked at her, noting her tear-swollen face. He'd never met Mrs. Pilgrim or even heard anything about her, but she dressed well, and her skirt and blouse were immaculate. During normal times, the Executioner doubted she'd allow such a pile of dirty tissues to build up around her. But these weren't normal times, she wasn't thinking straight, and he doubted that she'd even noticed the mess was there yet.

Georgia State Senator Henry Pilgrim looked little better. He didn't look as if he'd been crying, but the stress was visible in other ways. His white button-down shirt had been unbuttoned at the throat, and the cotton had darkened with sweat. A spot of something yellow—maybe mustard—stood out on his striped necktie, and the veins around his temples were throbbing and looked as if they might burst at any second.

"Listen up!" Wilkerson called out in a loud voice, and all of the other voices in the room fell into silence. "This is Matt Cooper from the Justice Department, Rick Jessup from DEA and Mr. John Sampson. Sampson's fluent in Arabic, Farsi and Hebrew. There are some new developments that might tie this kidnapping into some other criminal behavior. That's why these guys were brought in." He waved a hand in the direction of the newcomers. "We don't have time to explain it all to you right now, so just take my word for it. Give Cooper and his men your *complete* cooperation. If what they ask for sounds odd or un-orthodox, do it anyway. They aren't going to be able to explain it all to you under these time constraints, either."

The heads around the living room all nodded. But many of the faces told Bolan that at least half of the agents were skeptical.

"First thing we do," Bolan announced, "is go around the room clockwise and find out everything you've done so far. My men will be with me, and if you've got any questions for me, or them, that would be the time to ask them. But don't be surprised, or offended, if we say we can't tell you."

Bolan strode purposefully and confidently toward the love seat where the Pilgrims sat. Experience had taught him that the family members of kidnap victims had it the roughest of any victims of crime. They were forced to stay at home, staring at the phone, and terrified by both its silence and its ring. He wanted the Pilgrims to feel more relaxed immediately. The brains of people frightened out of their wits often went blank from overload, or at least got spotty. And one or both of the Pilgrims might well have some tiny bit of information that they hadn't even thought of telling the Feds, state or local cops who had invaded their home.

And that information could be exactly what he needed to pick up the trail of the men who had taken their daughter.

The Executioner knelt on one knee in front of the couple. But before he could speak, Myra Pilgrim looked up at him and suddenly stopped sniffling. "You're going to save her."

"We're certainly going to do our best," Bolan said.

"No, I mean *you*. *You're* going to save her yourself. Don't ask me how I know because I can't explain it. But sometimes, I just know things."

Next to his wife, slightly behind her where she couldn't see him, Henry Pilgrim rolled his eyes and shook his head.

"I don't mean you as in plural, Mr. Cooper," Myra Pilgrim went on. "I mean you, as in you yourself. Somehow I just know it'll be you." She reached out, took Bolan's hand and squeezed it.

Bolan watched Henry Pilgrim out of the corner of his eye. The man still held his wife's right hand, and there was a Bible resting on its spine between the couple's legs. Henry might be skeptical of his wife's obvious belief that she sometimes had psychic powers, but he wasn't exhibiting any negative reaction to her lacing her fingers through Bolan's. So the Executioner squeezed her hand back and said, "Someone in this group is going to locate Sarah Ann, Mrs. Pilgrim, and get her back to you. It might be me and then it might not. But I promise you it'll be someone."

Bolan stood back up and shook hands with Henry Pilgrim. "When I talk to the kidnappers on the phone next time they call," he said, "it may sound harsh to you. Like I'm taunting them—maybe even daring them to kill your daughter. I'm not. Just believe me—I know this kind of men better than you do. Trust me. Okay?"

Henry Pilgrim was hesitant. Lines of worry creased his forehead as he stared at the man standing before him. When he hadn't spoken, or even indicated that he'd heard Bolan's words, his wife turned toward him and said, "Trust him, Henry. Again, I'm unable to explain to you how I know. But I know."

Henry Pilgrim finally nodded. Probably, Bolan thought, to get her to shut up about knowing things.

Bolan moved on to the coffee table where one of the computer men sat in front of his keyboard and screen. He was about to ask a question when one of the phones rang. It was a green phone on an end table and had been reserved for Sarah Ann Pilgrim's captors to contact the family.

One of the agents, wearing a navy-blue nylon windbreaker with the letters FBI stenciled across the back, started to reach for the phone.

"Stand down, Schovenic," Wilkerson said. He pointed toward Bolan. "Cooper handles that line from now on."

The man in the blue windbreaker sat back in his chair and blew air out between his clenched teeth.

Bolan walked swiftly across the room and lifted the green receiver from its cradle. "Hello," he said into the instrument.

There was a long pause, then a heavily accented voice on the other end said, "Who is this?"

"First," the Executioner said, "who is *this*? What's wrong? Didn't your mother teach you it was impolite not to introduce yourself first?"

"You are not the FBI agent to whom I have been talking," the same voice said.

Bolan silently nodded to himself. He remembered John

Sampson telling them about how the kidnappers had spoken English just a little too formally. "To whom" was correct grammar—the kind a person was taught in a schoolroom. But most native-born Americans would have said, "Who am I talking to?"

"Right you are," Bolan said. "I'm *not* the agent you've talked to previously. I'm the agent you're going to talk to *now.*"

"Then what is your name?" the voice demanded.

"There you go again," Bolan said. "Tsk, tsk. No manners at all." He drew in a deep, dramatic breath of disapproval. "You tell me your name first. Then I'll tell you mine."

There was another long pause, then the voice said, "I demand to speak to the same man with whom I spoke before."

"Well, pal," Bolan said, "you're out of luck." He glanced down at the blue windbreaker worn by the man who had first reached for the phone, then read the name tag pinned to the breast opposite the FBI crest. Schovenic, it said. "Special Agent Schovenic's on his way to the hospital in the back of an ambulance right now. Heart attack." He paused a second, then added, "Probably your fault."

"Heart attack? I do not believe you."

"Then don't believe me," Bolan countered. "But that's the way it is. You talk to me now, or nobody." He paused only a second, giving his words time to sink in but not so much time that they'd lose the distraction he hoped they'd caused in the caller's mind. "Now, for the third time, what's your name?"

"Moe," the accented voice said. "You may refer to me as Moe."

"Okay," the Executioner said. "But tell me, Moe. Is that short for Mohammed? Or were your parents big Three Stooges fans?" He waited for the answer, knowing it couldn't help but anger the caller if he was familiar with the Three Stooges. And even if he didn't know them from Adam and Eve, he'd at least be confused and off balance.

"I do not know these Three Stooges of whom you speak. I am—"

"Never mind," the Executioner said. "You can call me

Cooper. But Cooper is really too tough for you, Moe, just call me Larry or Curly."

Yet a third long silence met Bolan's ears, and he could practically see the man on the other end of the line trying to figure out what that meant. He'd already said he hadn't heard of the Three Stooges, so he certainly wouldn't recognize their names.

Or would he? Was this accent and everything else just an act? Bolan still hadn't ruled out that possibility. He was dealing with very intelligent men. They could easily be smart enough to realize that they shouldn't have known much, if anything, about the Three Stooges if they'd grown up in the Middle East.

During this brief interim, Wilkerson hurried to Bolan's side and motioned for him to cover the receiver with his hand. Bolan did so, and then the FBI SAC said, "You're pushing them pretty hard. Making them mad would be my guess."

"I want them mad," Bolan whispered back. "Angry men make mistakes. And we need them to make a mistake."

The voice on the other end suddenly came back to life. Bolan waved Wilkerson back, then listened as Moe said, "My associates and I will have to talk over these new developments. We will call back in exactly one hour. If you do not answer by the third ring, we will kill the girl." This time, instead of silence, Moe separated his sentences with a laugh that managed to be both lewd and ghoulish at the same time. "Of course, we will not kill her until we have had a little fun with her first."

Anger boiled up inside the Executioner. Almost every cell in his body told him to lash out and tell Moe that he'd personally kill them all if they laid even one hand on Sarah Ann Pilgrim. But he couldn't risk such a loss of temper.

At least not yet.

"Well, you just go ahead and call back then," he said. "We don't really have any other plans for the day. We'll be here— probably watching a little TV or something."

Before Moe could answer, Bolan hung up.

THE GREEN PHONE RANG AGAIN exactly sixty minutes later.

Bolan picked up the phone. "Cooper here."

The man calling himself Moe said, "Do you have the money yet?"

They didn't. But Bolan said, "Of course we do."

"Then you are to place it into a large, strong, hard-sided suitcase. Then you must wrap the suitcase completely with duct tape to reinforce the snaps."

Bolan was taking notes as he listened. Whatever this man's plan was, it included the suitcase taking quite a beating. He wondered exactly what it might be, but before he could form any conclusions Moe went on. "Then you are to drive to the airport with the money and rent a private plane and pilot."

"That doesn't sound like it should be too hard," Bolan said.

"It will not be," Moe said.

Then, changing the subject, he said, "Tell me, Cooper. Was it you in that bright yellow monstrosity in the Oklahoma panhandle?"

"Of course it was," Bolan retorted. "Another ten seconds and I'd have had you."

"But it was not the girl you were after then," Moe said in a confident tone of voice. "It was the money."

"Good night," the Executioner said in mock amazement. "Will you look at the big brain on Moe. That's right. We'd already gotten the coke. Another ten seconds and we'd have had your money, and your asses."

Moe didn't respond for a second. When he finally did, he said, "Do you understand all that you are to do in packing the money?"

Bolan understood—more than Moe thought. They were going to toss the suitcase out somewhere during a flight. "I'm with you so far," the Executioner said. "What do we do then?"

"That is enough for now," Moe said. "You will be contacted by one of my men sometime after you reach the airport. You will get further instructions from him." He paused, then added,

"Need I tell you that if you attempt to take him into custody, or interfere with him in any way, the girl will be killed?"

"No, I could have pretty much figured that one out by myself," Bolan said.

"Good," Moe said. "Then we will speak again later."

Bolan heard the phone click in his ear. He turned toward Jessup, Sampson and Wilkerson. "Put somebody in charge here, Wilkerson. The four of us have got a money drop to make."

"But we don't have any money," Wilkerson protested. "Let alone a million dollars."

"I know that," Bolan explained. "But they don't know it."

Ever since Bolan had spoken to Myra Pilgrim, the woman had appeared to have come out of her zombielike state. When he looked her way now, the Executioner saw that she had even cleaned up the mess of used tissues around her feet and disposed of them. When he caught her eye, Bolan said, "Mrs. Pilgrim, do you have a large, hard-sided suitcase we could use?"

"I do," the lady said. "I'll go get it for you right now." She stood up and walked swiftly out of sight down a hallway.

"Jessup," Bolan said, "go with her and help her carry it. And find some old newspapers or magazines or both to fill it with. I don't know exactly how or when this thing is going to go down, but it might be important to make it feel heavy enough to hold a million bucks."

Jessup nodded and hurried down the hall after Mrs. Pilgrim.

Henry was on his feet now, too. "What can I do to help?" he asked.

"You have any duct tape, Henry?" the Executioner asked.

"Sure do," the Georgia state senator said. "You want gray or black?"

"Bring both. We're going to use a lot of it." Although he didn't want to say it out loud in front of the Pilgrims, he intended to tape the suitcase with every piece of tape he could find in the house. The more tape they had to cut through, the more time it would take. And the more time it took, the longer Sarah Ann Pilgrim was likely to stay alive.

Bolan turned back to Wilkerson as Henry hurried through a doorway into the kitchen. "Spec," he said, "did you put anyone else in charge here yet? I'm assuming you'd like to come with us."

"Wouldn't miss it for the world," the FBI man said.

"They're your men, so you choose. But if it were me, I'd hand the reins over to Schovenic. He's had the most experience talking with these human grub worms, and this Moe idiot seemed to get along with him well."

"I agree," Wilkerson said, "but I see a problem. He was taken to the hospital for a heart attack, remember?"

Bolan remembered. "Lucky man, that Schovenic," he said. "Turned out to be nothing more than a bad case of indigestion. Doctors sent him back home. Or, rather, back here."

The FBI SAC looked across the room to where Schovenic still sat. "Bill, you get all that?"

Schovenic nodded. "I'm in charge while you're gone," he said. "Been to the hospital emergency room, no heart attack, back now."

"You've got it," Bolan said.

By now Myra Pilgrim had led Rick Jessup—who had to use both hands to lug a huge gray suitcase—back to the living room. "It's already filled," the DEA agent said. "Thank goodness for *Sports Illustrated* and *Quilter's Monthly*. Our friends the Pilgrims here must have every issue of both magazines for the last ten years."

By now, Myra had practically gone through a transfiguration. She not only had quit crying, but she was also beaming with hope. "The quilting magazines are mine," she told Bolan just as Henry emerged from the kitchen with two brand-new rolls of duct tape. "*Sports Illustrated* is his. But I think he just subscribes to get the swimsuit issue."

Myra Pilgrim's remark brought several chuckles to lighten what had been a room of true gloom when Bolan, Sampson and Jessup first arrived. But Henry, who had returned too late to hear the whole story just said, "Huh?" with a blank look on his face.

Bolan knew it was the sudden activity that had lightened the atmosphere. And as several of the agents and cops began taping the suitcase, he moved quietly to where Schovenic sat. Leaning down, he whispered, "Sorry to pull your negotiating rug out from under your feet."

Schovenic waved a hand in front of his face. "No sweat, Cooper. The important thing is getting this girl back alive and in one piece."

Bolan nodded and stood erect. By now, the suitcase had been thoroughly taped and was ready. "Okay," the Executioner said. "Jessup, Wilkerson, Sampson and I are heading for the airport. We don't have to charter a private plane when we get there because we've already got one waiting. That's all we know so far. So hang loose but think tight. There's always a chance we may need to call back here for some kind of info or for backup."

The heads around the room nodded.

Henry and Myra Pilgrim walked over to Bolan. Henry stuck out his hand and said, "Thank you, Mr. Cooper."

Then Myra threw her arms around Bolan's neck and hugged him. "Bring my baby back to me," she said.

Bolan just nodded. Then he, Jessup, Sampson and Wilkerson left the house through the same door they'd come in.

BOLAN, RIDING SHOTGUN next to Wilkerson, turned in his seat and rested his arm on the back. "Someone's supposed to contact us while we're out here. But I don't know who, how or when. The only fly in the ointment is that it could be during the chartering process—the paperwork. It might even be the pilot. So, Jessup, I want you to go through the motions and rent us a plane."

Bolan reached into his right front pocket and pulled out a roll of bills. Counting off twenty hundreds, he handed them to the DEA agent in the backseat. "This ought to get the ball rolling. And stick with the pilot until you get back to the hangars. I don't think he'll be one of the bad guys because if the exchange is going to go down the way I'm guessing they have it planned, it would leave us holding their man."

"But we're actually taking *our* plane, right?" Jessup said. "With Jack flying?"

"Right," Bolan said. "Chartering another plane is just to play safe with whoever our contact is supposed to be."

Wilkerson turned the FBI sedan into the airport and drove directly around the perimeter road to the private planes' runways. An office building was set just off the asphalt with a sign in the window that read Day Or Night Charter Flights. The FBI SAC stopped the car and let Jessup out.

Bolan turned his head toward the long row of metal hangars in the distance and saw a man leaning against the corrugated steel wall of the closest one, smoking a cigarette. He wore OD-green BDUs, no visible weapons, and looked to be a National Guardsman or some other noncombatant military official.

Ten minutes later Jessup came back out of the office building with a man who looked to be in his midsixties. He was short and wiry, and wore a leather jacket similar to Grimaldi's trademark coat. A baseball cap that said Day Or Night Charter Flights sat atop his head with short curly gray hair sticking out of the cap from the back and sides. Jessup opened the door for him. The older man frowned as the DEA agent practically pushed him into the backseat. He was still frowning as Jessup got in and closed the door.

"To the hangars, Special," Jessup said as if Wilkerson were his chauffeur.

Trapped now between Sampson and Jessup, with Bolan and Wilkerson in the front seat, the gray-haired man looked more uneasy than ever. Finally, he worked up the courage to say, "You told us inside that you wanted the standard sightseeing tour. But you guys don't look like sightseers to me. Is this some kind of dope run? I don't want any part of it if it is."

Bolan suppressed a smile. He supposed they did look like a considerably rougher crew than the families this old man was used to flying around. So the Executioner pulled out his Justice Department credentials at the same time Wilkerson flipped his FBI badge out and over the seat. Jessup had done the same with his DEA credentials.

"Hot damn!" the old man said. "DEA, FBI and the U.S.

Justice Department?" He turned to Sampson. "You got a badge of some kind, too? Border Patrol or something? Listen, if you're IRS I can explain—"

"You don't have to explain anything," Bolan said as he dropped the leather case back into his pocket. "We'll explain what we can to you in a minute. But for the time being, keep in mind that you aren't in any danger. What's your name?"

"Burt," the man said. "Major Burt Dunbar, USAF retired."

"Great," Bolan said. "Okay, Burt. We've got a fairly complex deal going down—"

"Dope?" Dunbar said again.

"No, Burt, it doesn't have anything to do with dope," Bolan said patiently as Wilkerson drove toward the hangars. He had called ahead on his cell phone and knew Grimaldi would have the Learjet 60 warmed up and ready. "It's a kidnapping case. In the trunk of this car, we've got a suitcase that's supposed to be the ransom money."

"Hot damn!" Dunbar said. "But what do you want with me?"

Bolan explained how an unknown party was to make contact with them and give further instructions after they reached the airport.

"So let me get this straight," Dunbar said. "You were afraid I might be one of the bad guys, right?" His chest puffed out a little, and Bolan could see that at his age, still looking dangerous enough to be a kidnapper was a compliment. The Executioner hated to burst his bubble, so instead of telling him the truth, he said, "We still can't be sure you aren't. I mean, you might just be a really good actor who's pretending to just be a charter pilot."

There was no harm in letting a little old man feel young and spry for a while again.

The Executioner continued, "Since we can't be sure of you, the only alternative we have is to tape your hands and feet together and leave you in your plane while we take our own." He held up what was left of one of the duct tape rolls. "We'll radio back as soon as we're far enough away, and make sure someone comes out to get you."

"Hot damn!" Dunbar said for the third time. "There's another way, boys."

"And what's that?" Bolan asked.

Dunbar's face had almost begun to glow with excitement. It looked as if half of the wrinkles in his face had disappeared, and his pale blue eyes had widened. "Take me with you," he said.

Bolan looked over at Wilkerson as the FBI man shrugged. "Suits me," he said.

Turning his attention into the backseat, the Executioner saw Jessup nodding. There was something likable about the retired USAF man.

Sampson proved it a second later when he looked down to the man in the middle of the backseat and said, "You really want to go with us?"

"Sure do," Dunbar said.

"Then hot damn!" Sampson replied. "I think you should."

HARRY DRAKE KILLED HIS LATEST cell phone, then wiped it clean of fingerprints with the tail of his OD BDU blouse. Still holding the phone through the thin material, he pushed the button to roll down the Nissan Maxima window with the other hand, then tossed the instrument out of the vehicle.

Let them try to track me down all they want, Drake thought as he reached into the briefcase on the floor next to his feet and pulled out another fresh, prepaid and untraceable phone. One phone, one call, and keep moving. That was his motto during all of the fund-raising missions he and his men had been on, and so far it had worked every bit as well as he'd known it would. No one had connected him with any of the phone calls to the Pilgrim house.

Dropping the new phone into the right breast pocket of his fatigue blouse, he heard the rattle of the pills in the bottle on the other side of his chest. He glanced at his watch. It was still a little early for another dose. But who knew what he might be tied up in when the time to take more Xanax and Lortab came? Opening the bottle, he popped one of each of the pills into his mouth, washing them down with a swig of whiskey from the same briefcase from which he'd pulled the new cell phone.

Ahead, Drake could see that they were approaching the airport. And from the trunk came the same constant, monotonous bumping sound he'd heard ever since they'd tossed the bound and gagged Sarah Ann Pilgrim into the rear of the car and slammed the door on her. But the noise didn't worry him. It wasn't loud enough for anyone outside the vehicle to hear it while the automobile was in motion, and when they reached the Cessna in the private hangars it would take only a second to transfer the little bitch onto the plane.

Drake felt a smile curling the ends of his mouth. What they were about to do was not only going to finally net them enough money to purchase the specific items he wanted, but it was going to be fun, as well.

Drake was riding shotgun for Felix Bundy, who was behind the Maxima's wheel. In the backseat were Sal Whitlow and Don O'Hara. Right about now Joe Knox, the retired British SAS pilot, would be warming up the Cessna they had stolen in Canada and repainted with phony numbers and other regalia.

And the two former USMC recons, Elmer Scott and Charlie Ducket, should be nearing the coordinates where they'd be waiting on the ground.

Everything was going like clockwork, and Harry Drake's smile grew even wider. He had broken the team into two parts only once before during this string of criminal activities, when they'd done the kidnapping and robbery in Wilmer, Minnesota, and Boston. But it had worked well then, and it would work well again this time.

This would be the final step before the buy he had in mind. Then, instead of the parents of a teenage girl, he would demand money from the U.S. government itself. And it would not be a million dollars he'd saddle them with.

It would be a *billion*.

Drake turned back to the front as they entered the gate to the airport and took a right toward the runways and hangars reserved for private planes. As soon as they reached the first corrugated-steel building, Bundy slowed the car, then stopped.

"You're on, Whitlow," Drake said as his fellow ex-Green Beret got out of the car. He had picked Whitlow to be the man who actually made contact with the Feds for two reasons. First, he had the darkest skin of any of Drake's men, and he had a slightly hooked nose, which betrayed Arab blood somewhere back on one of the distant branches of his family tree. The second reason was that he had the best phony Middle-Eastern accent of any of them, including Drake.

As soon as Whitlow had closed the door behind him, Bundy switched his foot from the brake back to the accelerator. Slowly, the Maxima drove past the open stalls. A few were empty, but most had planes of one kind or another waiting inside them. About halfway down the row, Drake even saw a pilot warming up his Learjet. The man wore a well-worn brown leather bomber jacket and a suede cap. He was reading a paperback book but looked up briefly as Drake and his handpicked crew of ex-military criminals passed.

Drake nodded. The pilot had former military written all over him.

The Cessna had been pulled into the last hangar in line and, like the Learjet, was warming up in preparation for flying. There was even a pilot sitting behind the controls of the propeller craft, but it wasn't the guy in the leather jacket and cap this time. Instead, it was former SAS commando pilot Joe Knox.

Felix Bundy stopped just past the last hangar, twisted the wheel as far as it would go and backed the Maxima into the hangar until the vehicle's bumper was almost touching the propeller. Then the men got out of the truck.

Their arms, equipment and other supplies had already been loaded, so the only "parcel" that had to be taken from the car to the plane was Sarah Ann Pilgrim. Drake ducked under the prop and inserted a key into the trunk lock. A second later the trunk was open and he looked in to see that his captive was still tied securely at both the wrists and ankles. She lay on her right side, a ball gag stuffed into her mouth so she couldn't speak.

But as soon as she saw light from the open trunk she began making strange, half growling, half pleading sounds, at the same time kicking both of her feet back and forth.

Felix Bundy stood on the other side of the trunk, looking in.

"Grab her by the shoulders," Drake ordered as he reached in and grasped the girl's kicking feet. Together, they lifted her out of the trunk and carried her to the door of the Cessna Conquest I.

Drake took his seat next to Knox while the rest of his men got Sarah Ann settled in a seat in the back. She had stopped fighting now and replaced her resistance with huge tears running down her cheeks. Through the ball gag she began to make a whimpering, mewing sound.

The sound had the same effect on Drake as the screech of fingernails drawn down a chalkboard. He was sick and tired of the little bitch, and happy as hell that he'd be rid of her soon. She was enough to make the former Green Beret sergeant believe he was being underpaid for the job. It should have been worth far more than a million dollars for him to listen to her over the past two days.

"We ready to go, chappie?" Joe Knox said in his English accent.

"Uh-uh," Drake said. "The money car hasn't even arrived yet. Just stick the nose out far enough that we can see where Whitlow's going to stop them."

Knox complied, easing the Cessna 425's cabin just far enough past the metal walls that they could see down the line toward the charter office. Whitlow was right where he was supposed to be, waiting with his ever-present unfiltered cigarette hanging from his lips.

Pulling a small walkie-talkie from the pocket of his BDU blouse, Drake pressed the button on the side and said, "D to W. D to W. Come in, W."

"W here, loud and clear," Whitlow's voice came back over the walkie-talkie. "Hey, nice little poem, huh?"

"Shut up and get serious, you jackass," Drake growled at him. "The men you're about to deal with have already proved they're damn good at putting gunmen in their graves. You aren't dealing with bank tellers this time. These guys would like nothing better than to put a few bullets in your brain and get the little bitch back for free. Particularly that Cooper bastard. There's something about him that worries me."

"What?" Whitlow asked.

"I don't know," Drake said. "Just something about him. We've got the definite advantage over most law enforcement because they have to play by the rules. We don't. But there's something about Cooper that makes me suspect he might be willing to bend a few rules himself to get the job done. I've got a feeling that he's more than willing to get down in the trenches with us and fight as dirty as he has to."

"Could be, D," Whitlow said in a far less gregarious tone of voice. "But let's not let him spook us. When it comes to dirty fighting, we've still got him way outnumbered."

"Have you seen any sign of them yet, W?" Drake asked. He was tired of even thinking about Cooper, let alone talking about him. Besides, even if the bastard was Superman himself, they were far too committed at this point to cancel their plans now.

"I'm not sure, D," Whitlow said. "But there's a black sedan I can see following the perimeter road and coming our way. So many antennae are sticking out of the damn thing it looks like my grandma Maudie's pincushion."

"Affirmative, W," Drake said. "You know what to tell them. Just keep us advised. In fact—" He cut himself off in midsentence, thinking. Timing was crucial at this stage. He didn't want the men delivering the money to know he, his men and Sarah Ann Pilgrim were all on the ground and less than a hundred yards away when Whitlow stopped them. The FBI would have sent either one of their SWAT teams or their hostage and rescue squad, and guys like that were likely to try to take the girl before the Cessna could get airborne.

That could get messy. At this point, on the ground with his men divided into two groups, what Whitlow had said about outnumbering Cooper and the FBI didn't hold water. Right now,

Drake and his men would be outnumbered and outgunned. And they'd lose the battle.

Which meant they'd lose their lives along with it.

"Sir?" Whitlow said. "Sir? Are you still there?"

"I'm here, W," Drake said, realizing he had let the airwaves go silent while he thought.

"W, I want you to stop them before they get to the first hangar. Go ahead and give them the slip of paper I gave you. But don't give them their other directions until we've passed you and started down the runway." He paused and smiled to himself again. "I want to taxi right past the sons of bitches. I want them to see us before they know who we are, and watch us take off, and then find out that they had their chance and blew it. Make sure they know it was us, W. If it doesn't look like they've figured it out for themselves, then you *tell* them. You got that?"

"Got it," Whitlow said into the walkie-talkie. "Anything else?"

"That should do it for now," Drake said. "Just make sure they know they were only inches away from us and the girl, and tell them they'll get further instructions from me once we're all in the air."

"Will do, sir," Whitlow said. "W out."

Drake lifted his thumb off the walkie-talkie as the man he'd seen go into the charter office came back out with a smaller, older man. They both got into the black vehicle covered with antennae and drove slowly toward the row of hangars.

"Let's go, Joe," Drake said to his pilot.

Knox guided the Cessna the rest of the way out of the hangar, then turned.

Drake watched the FBI car stop in front of Sal Whitlow's outstretched palm, and gave the men inside the sedan a big smile as the Cessna passed them.

Thirty seconds later, they had reached the runway, received radio clearance for takeoff and were racing down the tarmac.

4

Bolan watched the man in the BDUs throw down his cigarette as the FBI vehicle approached. A second later, he stuck out his hand, his palm facing the black sedan.

At that precise moment the Executioner realized this was to be the contact of which Moe had spoken. The guy in the green fatigues was no National Guardsman. He was one of the terrorists. In addition to the Nam leaf-camouflage fatigues they had reportedly worn during robberies and other crimes, they obviously had plain OD BDUs when they wanted to attract less attention.

In today's America, with war raging in the Middle East and Islamic extremists continuing their covert operations in the States, National Guard uniforms made even less of a lasting impression than police uniforms.

Bolan leaned over toward the driver's side of the vehicle as Wilkerson stopped just in front of the man's outstretched hand. "You the one who's supposed to meet us?" the FBI man asked.

"Yes, it is I," a very heavily accented voice answered.

Bolan leaned over even farther so he could look at the young man's face. All the skin not covered by his fatigues was a light brown. His features looked somewhat Arabic, but his coloring could also have come from being part American Indian, Mexican or South American.

"Well, then," Bolan said, doing his best to keep all skepticism out of his voice, "tell us what we're supposed to do next."

As the Executioner spoke, a Cessna Model 425 Conquest II rolled out of its hangar at the end of the long line of metal shelters. The business craft began taxiing their way.

"Wait one moment," said the man with the accent, "until this plane has passed us and the noise is gone."

Bolan and the rest of the men waited. A few seconds later, the Cessna passed. The man in the seat next to the pilot gave them a big smile and a wave.

Bolan nodded back. It took a few seconds, but then something clicked in his brain, and somehow he suddenly knew it had been the kidnappers in the Cessna. He twisted farther, and saw the Cessna reach the runway and start down the tarmac. His hand shot instinctively to the .44 Magnum Desert Eagle on his hip but stopped on the grips.

It was too late now to take them down before they left the ground. And the Executioner's first priority had to be saving the girl's life, not shooting her by mistake. Killing or capturing the vermin who had kidnapped her had to be pushed back to second place. Their time would come—Bolan would make sure of it.

But regardless of how close to him the young woman had probably just been that time wasn't now.

Now that the Cessna was safely out of range, the man at the window spoke again. "In case you have not figured it out for yourselves, those were my associates on that airplane," he said in the same thick accent. "Sarah Ann Pilgrim is on the airplane with them. You are to take off on the same runway as the Cessna just did, then set a course due north. The men in the Cessna will contact you on this frequency and give you further orders." He shoved a folded piece of paper through the window to Wilkerson, who passed it on to Bolan.

The Executioner unfolded it, glanced down at the numbers, then folded it again and stuck it in his pocket. He'd give the frequency to Jack Grimaldi so he could program it into the plane's radio as soon as they boarded the Learjet.

A sudden long shot occurred to the Executioner, and he decided he had nothing to lose by trying it. His right hand was still on the grips of the Desert Eagle, and he pulled the huge pistol out of its Concealex holster and aimed it past Wilkerson's face toward the man in the green BDUs. "Suppose I decide to just kill you here and now?" he growled in a low, menacing voice.

The dark-skinned man shrugged, then lifted the walkie-talkie that had been hidden below the car door until then.

Bolan could see that his thumb was pressing the transmit button.

"They are listening to every word we say," said the dark-skinned man outside the sedan. "If they hear a shot, or any other indication that you have harmed me, they will kill the girl. And after they have killed her, do not be surprised if they hunt you each up in your bedroom some night, and cut your throats or put a bullet in your head while you sleep. That will be *after* they have killed your wives and sons and daughters, of course." The Middle-Eastern accent seemed to be getting stronger as the conversation continued.

Bolan wasn't sure exactly what to make of that. But he had to admit that former 101st Airborne paratrooper John Sampson had been right. The accent sounded phony, as if the man was trying just a little too hard to sound Arabic or Iranian.

Without another word, the Executioner holstered the .44 and motioned for Wilkerson to drive on.

The FBI SAC rolled the window back up as the sedan started down the hangars toward the Learjet. Grimaldi had already rolled it out onto the tarmac by the time they reached where he'd been parked. Bolan, Jessup, Sampson and Burt Dunbar hurriedly loaded a few things from the car into the aircraft. Then Wilkerson drove it on past the hangars to a small parking lot before jogging back.

"Let's get a move on, Jack," the Executioner said as he buckled himself in. "I'll fill you in on what's happening while we fly."

"Man," Grimaldi said as he taxied the Learjet full speed past the hangars and the man in the green BDUs. "If I had a dime for every time I've heard you say that, I'd retire to some beach in the South of France where the women don't wear tops to their bikinis."

As soon as they were off the ground, Grimaldi set his course

due north as the terrorist in the plain OD BDUs had instructed.
Bolan handed his pilot the piece of paper with the radio frequency number written on it, and Grimaldi practically laughed
out loud. "Man, nobody uses that one anymore," he said. "Too
much weather interference. It's a good choice by the bad guys,
though. There's not likely to be anyone else listening in." As
the jet leveled off he reached forward, set the controls on au-
topilot, then began programming the little-used frequency into
the digital radio.

Straight from the factory, the Learjet 60 had seated eleven
passengers. But this one had been completely remodeled under
the guidance of John "Cowboy" Kissinger, and four of the seats
had been removed. The back of the cabin had been turned into
a cargo and conference area, with a round table and four chairs
bolted to the deck. The walls were covered with lockers not
unlike those you might find in the dressing room of a professional football team. But instead of helmets, shoulder pads and
jock straps, they contained weapons, ammunition, a wide variety
of clothing, disguise elements and communications equipment.

Bolan looked behind him and saw that Sampson now sat
behind Grimaldi, with Jessup across the aisle behind him.
Between Bolan and Jessup, a wildly smiling Burt Dunbar was
looking for the short end of his own seat belt. The elderly man
looked like a Little Leaguer who had just tapped one over the
fence and was circling the bases in victory.

Jessup was watching Dunbar, too, and the old man's enthu-
siasm had brought a smile to the DEA agent's face. "You having
a good time, Burt?" he asked.

Dunbar finally found the belt and clipped it together across his
lap. "Ain't had so much fun since the pigs ate my little brother,"
he said. "Most days I fly the most boring people you could imagine
around, and listen to the most boring things a man could hear."

"You talk back to them?" Jessup asked as Grimaldi continued to work on the radio.

"You better believe I do." Dunbar grinned. "And I've learned
to be just as boring as they are when I want to be."

As they continued to rise in the air, Grimaldi finished programming the radio, then said, "Hello, boys," into the microphone.

Bolan laughed softly to himself. Grimaldi was violating FAA regulations by ignoring signal codes and other formalities. But they had also taken off without clearance, luckily not running head-on into any other planes leaving or arriving at Atlanta.

"Hello," came a heavily accented voice over the radio. "And welcome to the friendly skies. We hope you are having a pleasant flight."

Behind the Executioner, Bolan sensed that Sampson had leaned forward. "You hear that accent? That guy, and the one we talked to through the window. Their accents aren't like any I've ever heard before. At least not in Iran. To be honest with you, it sounds like an American who's trying to sound like English is a second language. It's…well…overdone."

Bolan nodded. Reaching over, he took the mike from Grimaldi and said, "Who am I speaking to?"

"Ah, it is you, Mr. Cooper," the same accented voice said. "The last time we spoke you lectured me on telephone etiquette. Does not the same rule apply when using a radio?"

Grimaldi had leveled the plane off and was continuing the flight north. Bolan looked down and saw that they were flying over the Coosa River. "Please accept my apology," he said into the mike. "Yes, this is Cooper. And you must be Moe."

"Correct," said the voice on the radio. "Short for Mohammed. Not your Three Stooges or the Marx Brothers or—" Moe quit talking suddenly, as if he had just caught himself giving away information he didn't want the Executioner to have.

"You still there, Moe?" Bolan asked after several seconds of silence.

"I am here," Moe came back, the accent even stronger this time.

"See what I mean?" Sampson whispered even though Bolan had let up on the transmit button. "That accent is so good it sounds fake. Forced."

Bolan nodded. He was beginning to think they were onto something. Pushing the button again, he said, "Your man on the ground said you'd have further instructions for us once we were in the air. So tell us what to do and we'll do it."

Moe laughed over the airwaves. "Do you have the money with you?"

"Of course we do," the Executioner said. "If I'm not mistaken, trading you the money for Sarah Ann Pilgrim was the whole reason for this elaborate dog-and-pony show." He paused to take a breath, then went on. "It's safely packed in a hard-sided suitcase. You know? The kind that the gorillas jump up and down on in TV commercials?"

A short silence allowed the radio to pop and crack with interference. Then Moe said, "I have not seen this thing. Is the suitcase taped as I ordered?"

"Oh, yes," said the Executioner in a bored tone. "We're following all of your orders to the letter, you little potentate, you." The comment was designed to irritate Moe again as Bolan had done earlier at the house. But if the terrorist was growing angry, he didn't show it. His voice was still low and even when he said, "Tell your pilot to change course."

"To what?" Grimaldi asked as Bolan held the microphone in front of his face.

Moe read off a set of numbers, and Grimaldi made a few adjustments on the panel in front of him.

"We will stop talking for a while now," Moe said. "I will contact you again when it is time to change courses once more."

"We'll be waiting," the Executioner said. He let up on the button and hooked the mike back into the clip next to the radio. Turning in his seat, he saw Jessup, Sampson and Dunbar all looking his way.

The Executioner cleared his throat. "Guys, this is going to get hairy before it's all over. If any of you want out, there's no shame in it." He glanced at Dunbar out of the corner of his eye, then Sampson. Neither man had moved and stared stone-faced back at him.

"Okay," the gray-haired former USAF major said. "I know you're thinking this old man can't cut the mustard anymore.

And all he was was a flyboy in the first place." He coughed, then stuck his chest out almost like a bodybuilder posing on stage. "I may be worn-out, but I can still pull the trigger on a gun. And I'd rather go down swinging than give it up in a hospital bed hooked up to a bunch of damn hoses and IVs and breathing contraptions and such." He paused briefly. "So the only way you're getting rid of me is to shoot me."

Bolan smiled and turned to Sampson. The white-haired man said, "I'm in, too. My kids are all grown and have families of their own. And my wife started divorce proceedings a couple of months ago. I'm not suicidal, but I really don't care at this point if I live or die. Do you know what I mean?"

Bolan nodded. Like the samurai of feudal Japan, he had considered himself a walking dead man ever since he'd taken up his one-man war against evil. He had lived by the sword, using it to cut swatches through hordes of Mafia, Soviet KGB, criminals and terrorists. He knew that someday his own number would come up, and by the sword he would die.

But the Executioner planned to draw his last breath while in the process of trying to save someone else.

To his side, Bolan heard Moe and Grimaldi on the radio again, changing courses. He turned back around in his seat and settled in. Glancing out and down again, he saw a small village that looked as if it had come straight out of *Gone with the Wind*. Huge mansions dotted the rolling hills and dales of cotton and tobacco plantations.

"Sounds like we're all in this together, then," Sampson said behind him.

BELOW, BOLAN COULD SEE what he was sure had to be Charlotte, North Carolina. Far to the west, the Appalachian Mountains rose from the earth. They had not heard from Moe in almost an hour, and the biggest challenge Grimaldi had faced was keeping the Learjet in the air at a speed slow enough that it didn't overtake the Cessna.

Then, out of the blue, the radio sparked out static and Moe

came back on. "Gentlemen," he said in his overdone accent, "it is almost time for the exchange."

Bolan lifted the microphone out of the clip but didn't reply.

A second later, Moe said, "Did you hear me, Cooper?"

"I heard you," the Executioner acknowledged. "It was a statement rather than a question so I didn't answer you."

Moe's voice sounded more like the low growl of an angry dog when he said, "It will not happen today, Mr. Cooper. But I truly hope you and I can meet in person someday. I am sure it would be interesting."

"Oh, it's going to happen, and I promise you I'll make it interesting. Not very long, maybe, but interesting while it lasts."

"We will see," Moe said. "Now, it is almost time for you to give us our money."

"And just how do you plan for us to do that?" the Executioner asked. "We could pull up next to you, I guess. You want me to jump over to your plane, or would you rather jump over to mine?"

"You amuse yourself, I hope," Moe said. "But to me, you are not that funny."

"Then I'll play it straight," the Executioner said. "What do you have planned?"

"When I give the word—*exactly* when I give the word—you are to throw the suitcase out the door and let it drop."

"Oh," Bolan said. "I get it. You're going to be below us and catch it."

The angry growl came back, and Bolan knew he was getting on the man's nerves. Good. That's what he wanted. Men like this Moe character decided before the kidnapping itself even took place whether they were going to kill their hostage, and nothing Bolan could say would change that decision either way. But if he could continue to keep Moe rattled, the man just might make a mistake that created an advantage for the Executioner.

"We have personnel on the ground, Mr. Cooper," Moe said. "They will retrieve the suitcase and check it. Then, assuming everything is in order, you will turn around and return to Atlanta."

"What about Sarah Ann Pilgrim?" Bolan asked.

"She will remain with us for only a short time. We will touch down in a major city somewhere, release her unharmed, then fly away." Moe stopped speaking for a minute, then his near maniacal laughter mixed with the angry growl came back. "The whole country has been following this story on CNN, MSNBC and FOX. So I'm sure that the security police at whichever airport we pick will be more than happy to help her." He paused, then said, "Just in case, however, I will leave enough change with her to call you."

"That's very considerate of you, Moe," Bolan said.

Sampson leaned forward again and said excitedly, "Did you hear that? Did you hear him say he'd leave her with enough *change* to make a call? I've never heard an Iranian or Arab speaking English in my life who used that word. It's far too technical. If he had that much discernment of the English language, he'd have lost his accent along the way, too. Instead, his accent is stronger than if he'd never learned English at all." Sampson excitedly took another breath. "No, if he was really from the Middle East, he'd have said he'd leave her with enough *money* to call. I could be wrong, of course—there are exceptions to every rule. But I'd bet my oil company that this Moe character is as American as you or me. Might be English or Australian or even South African, I suppose. But my money's on his natural voice being a Texas drawl, a Brooklyn accent or sounding like some West Coast surferboy."

The Executioner nodded. "I think you're right," he said. "What I haven't figured out yet is why they're going to so much trouble to make us think they're from the Middle East."

Burt Dunbar was leaning forward now, too. "Could be just to throw us off. Lead us down the wrong trail, so to speak."

Turning toward Grimaldi, the Executioner said, "Jack, be sure to note our coordinates when we throw out the suitcase."

Grimaldi nodded. "Have you thought about what you're going to do when their men on the ground cut through all the duct tape and find old magazines instead of a million dollars?" he asked.

"I've thought about it," Bolan replied.

"So what *are* you going to do?" Grimaldi asked.

"I don't know," the Executioner said. "Not yet, at least."

Grimaldi had started speak again when Moe came back on the radio. "Drop time will be in ten seconds. *Exactly* ten seconds from the time I quit speaking. You must not be early or late. If you are, the money may easily be lost. And, of course, that means we will kill the girl."

Bolan keyed the mike. "I'm opening the door now," he said. He hooked the mike back on the dash, unbuckled his seat belt, stood up, then walked between the seats behind him to the side door.

The suitcase filled with old *Quilting Monthly* and *Sports Illustrated* magazines stood waiting on the deck. The Executioner reached out and slid the door open. The wind rushed in like a hurricane, blowing papers and everything else not nailed or bolted down around the rear of the cabin.

"Countdown starts now," Moe said over the radio. "Ten, nine, eight, seven, six…"

The Executioner scooted the heavy suitcase toward the opening. It was just wide enough to push it on through if he did so edgewise.

"Five, four, three, two," Moe said.

Bolan inched the heavy suitcase a third of the way on out of the partially opened door. The wind whipped around it, creating a vacuum that threatened to pull it out of the door slit prematurely. The Executioner gripped the sides of the suitcase with both hands, holding on with all of his strength, feeling the pectoral muscles in his chest bloat as the blood rushed into them.

Finally, the Executioner heard Moe say, "One…drop it!"

Bolan pushed the suitcase the rest of the way out of the plane, then grasped the handle and slid the door shut again. The papers, plastic cups, eating utensils and other light items blowing around the cabin suddenly settled.

The Executioner returned to his seat next to Grimaldi and sat down.

"We can see it falling," Moe said over the radio. "Continue

on this course behind us. As soon as we get word from our associates on the ground that they have the money, you will be released to return to Atlanta. Then we will proceed to release the girl as I have already promised you."

Bolan waited, wondering exactly what he would do when the men on the ground opened the suitcase and found magazines instead of money. "Speed up a little, Jack," he said as they waited. "I want to get a visual on that Cessna. Maybe we can even get a look inside. If Sarah Pilgrim isn't on board, we may even want to take these guys down from the air, so get your guns ready."

Grimaldi flipped a switch to retract the steel cover panels from the twin 60 mm machine guns hidden inside the Learjet.

"If we even *suspect* Sarah's on board," the Executioner cautioned, "that's no longer an option."

Grimaldi nodded his understanding.

The Learjet 60 increased its speed until the Cessna came into view ahead. It was a few hundred feet higher than the Learjet. But Jack Grimaldi didn't need to be told what to do. He lifted up on the control column and the jet shot up to an altitude a few hundred feet above the Cessna. Grimaldi increased speed and the jet shot past the slower, propeller-powered plane.

Bolan strained, looking down, trying to see through the windshield as they passed. But at the angle at which they were passing, all he could see were the blurred faces of a pilot and someone in the front passenger's seat. "Take her on up and cut a U-turn, Jack," the Executioner said.

Grimaldi nodded and the Learjet 60 shot forward again with another tremendous burst of speed. The pilot from Stony Man Farm kept it up for a good twenty seconds, then suddenly twisted the plane hard to the left. Bolan and the other men on board were all pressed tightly against the right side of the Cessna. But suddenly, they were flying back the way they had come.

For a moment, it looked as if the two planes would collide in midair. But a second before that could happen, Grimaldi took the Lear up and it passed quickly over the Cessna. The pressure caused by the Lear flying so close over the prop plane drove the Cessna several hundred feet downward, toward the earth.

And the radio went wild.

"What are you doing!" Moe screamed. In the background, the Executioner could hear other voices cursing and yelling. One scream—distinctively feminine—came blasting through the radio speaker, too.

It confirmed what Bolan thought he had seen when they'd just passed over the Cessna—a brief glimpse of a young woman with her hands together in her lap, and her ankles pressed tightly together. He hadn't seen ropes or handcuffs or tape or any other kind of restraints during the split-second view he had gotten.

But he knew they were there. The positioning of the wrists and ankles proved it.

Sarah Ann Pilgrim *was* on the plane, her hands and feet bound together.

There would be no shooting the Cessna down from the air.

"What are you doing!" Moe screamed over the radio again.

Bolan lifted the microphone for what seemed like the hundredth time since they'd begun following the Cessna. "Sorry about all that, Moe," he said. "Just wanted to get a little better look at you guys."

"Do it again and I will kill this girl immediately!" Moe shouted back.

"No, thanks," the Executioner said. "We're done." He directed Grimaldi to turn around yet again. The pilot complied, and they took up a position just above and behind the Cessna.

Five more minutes went by with the Executioner occasionally getting glimpses of the Atlantic Ocean to his right. They were continuing the northern route, but occasionally Moe would come back on the radio and give them a slightly different course. Bolan knew it was done just to keep them off balance.

Then finally, Moe came back on the radio, his voice filled with rage. "So you think this is some kind of joke?" he screamed, and his high-pitched voice threatened to shatter the eardrums of everyone in the Learjet. "You fill a suitcase with old magazines and think we will not open it before we release this woman?"

"Well, Moe," Bolan said, holding the mike up to his mouth again, "it was all I could think of to do. We didn't *have* a million dollars to give you." He felt his fingers tighten around the microphone. Now was the moment of truth. Within the next few seconds, he would find out if Sarah Ann Pilgrim would live or die.

"You have not heard the last from us," Moe screamed in his exaggerated accent. "And the blood of this young woman is on your hands!"

The radio suddenly went silent.

A moment later, through the windshield of the Learjet, Bolan saw a woman wearing a red dress—her hands and feet tied together—shoved out of the Cessna just below them.

A chill ran down the back of the Executioner's neck but it was caused by a sudden surge of adrenaline rather than fear. "Parachute!" he yelled at the top of his voice as he snapped open his seat belt.

Rounding the edge of his seat, he felt the air rush into the cargo area again as Burt Dunbar pulled the door open. Sprinting down the aisle between the seats, he could see Rick Jessup in front of one of the lockers bolted to the wall in the cargo area. He pulled out a prepacked parachute, turned and handed it to John Sampson.

By now the Executioner was only one step from the open door. He reached out, grabbing one of the chute's shoulder straps as Sampson shoved it his way.

With the unopened parachute clenched in his fist, Bolan never even broke stride as he raced out the door and into the open air thousands of feet above the earth.

At first, the blast of wind pulled him almost directly back from the door, past the Learjet's tail, and then away from the plane. Then he began to fall.

Bolan clenched the strap in his hand with an iron grip. It was the only thing that stood between him and certain death for both of the falling bodies.

As he continued to drop, the Executioner slid his arms through the chute pack's straps, then buckled the belt around his waist. With the parachute finally in place, he turned his eyes downward. Far, far below, he saw a faint red speck falling toward the ground, and the sight threatened to make him give up hope, then and there.

Bolan saw no way he could reach Sarah Ann Pilgrim before she smashed into the ground. Not considering the distance between them now.

But as soon as those negative thoughts entered his brain, the Executioner forced them out again. He didn't know if it was possible to still save the young woman. But as long as they were both alive, there was still a chance.

Reaching down toward his toes with his hands, he twisted into a jackknife dive so that he was now falling head-first. Keeping his arms tucked tightly to his sides and his legs pressed firmly together, the Executioner reduced his wind resistance. He could feel himself falling faster now, and the red speck, which he knew to be Sarah Ann Pilgrim's dress, grew slightly larger.

Seconds became a minute. Then one minute became two. But to the Executioner, each second felt like a decade. And to Sarah Ann Pilgrim, he suspected they would feel like centuries.

Finally, Bolan closed the gap to the point where the speck actually became a woman to his eyes. She was free-falling completely haphazardly, head up, head down, then from one side to the other. When her feet fell below her, the dress blew up and decreased her speed slightly. Head down made her go faster, and when she was on her sides the dress wrapped tightly around her and did no good then, either.

Bolan began closing the last few feet between them; the ground continued to rush toward his eyes at an alarming rate. He wasn't sure now that he could even open the chute for himself and get any good out of it. It might well be too late for them both.

But if it was, so be it. Again, as he had always known his own death would come, he would die at least trying to save some innocent man or woman.

Finally, the Executioner reached a point where he could reach down and touch the top of the young woman's up-stretched hair.

He had to be careful now. If he rammed down into her too hard, he might send her tumbling off in another direction.

And there would be no second chance. The ground was still coming toward them faster and faster.

Spreading his legs, Bolan slowed slightly, then grabbed a handful of hair. Sarah Ann Pilgrim shrieked slightly, then quieted. A second after that, Bolan had pulled her up, face-to-face with him.

Sarah modestly pushed her skirt back down between them, and the Executioner wrapped an arm around her waist. He reached to his side, pulling from his waistband the Cold Steel Caledonian Edge combat folding knife that Kissinger had given him. A flick of his thumb against the thumb stud was all it took to open the dagger-shaped blade, and then he brought the razor-sharp edge down through the tape that secured the woman's hands.

Sarah Ann Pilgrim immediately reached up and hugged her arms around his neck. Bolan tugged her closer to his own body, feeling her chest smash into his. Then, with the same hand that held the knife, he pulled the rip cord and the chute shot up above them.

Bolan folded the blade back into the knife and clipped it back into his waistband. He looked down. Below, he could see a cotton field ripe for picking. Then, as the chute opened and jerked them back up slightly, he wrapped his other arm around the young woman. She hugged him back even tighter, and he felt the wetness of her tears as she pressed her face into his neck and sobbed.

They could only have been a few hundred feet above the ground when the chute opened, and when they hit, they hit hard. But the Executioner tightened his grip on the young woman and controlled their roll, spreading the impact out across their bodies as much as was possible. A few seconds later, they rolled to a halt. Both suddenly found themselves on the ground in sitting positions, facing each other.

And the worst injuries they had were where the cotton stems had scratched their skin.

Sarah Ann Pilgrim stared wide-eyed and somewhat distantly at Bolan. "Are you an angel?" she asked, and it was obvious to Bolan that she wasn't kidding. "You've got to be," the young woman went on. "You've got to be an angel straight from God Himself."

Bolan grinned at her as he stood up, reached for her hand and helped her to her feet. "I can introduce you to a whole lot of people who wouldn't agree with that statement," he said as he lifted her in his arms and began carrying her out of the cotton field toward the nearest road.

5

Harry Drake was pissed. Not only had that government son of a bitch Cooper screwed him out of his million dollars, but the news reports also said that Sarah Ann Pilgrim had been saved by an unknown party who free-fell through the sky and caught her before she hit the ground. That had to be Cooper, too.

Who the hell *was* this guy, Superman?

Drake sat back against his seat in the Cessna, glancing for a second at Joe Knox, the former SAS pilot who was still manning the controls of the plane. They had turned due south after Drake had pushed the girl out of the door and now were approaching Key West, Florida, where they would touch down to refuel.

But refueling wasn't the only reason they were stopping over at Key West. Drake was also about to attend the most important meeting of his life. But unless he did some fast and fancy talking, that meeting showed every sign of concluding very badly.

Drake reached up and scratched the side of his face, feeling himself squint as he reflected on the recent events. He had expected the Learjet to land as close as possible to where he'd dumped the girl. Instead, he'd seen a flash of movement when Cooper had jumped out after her. He'd caught a glimpse of the man as he struggled into his parachute while falling through the air, then lost sight of him. Instead of landing, though, the Learjet had followed him for a few miles, then turned back. Why the much-faster aircraft had done that he didn't know. But it had.

Now, as Knox brought the Cessna down onto the runway at Key West, Drake sat silently in his seat. The man he was about to meet had been an elite soldier just like Drake and his men. The only difference was that all of Drake's crew came from either the U.S. or Great Britain, and the man with whom he was to meet had served on the other side of the iron curtain.

Alexi Kudinov had been a Spetsnaz sergeant before the fall of the Soviet Union. And he had made off with some very interesting souvenirs during the tumultuous period of transition. He had been selling everything from AK-47s and Tokarev pistols to tanks and fighter jets since that time. But he had kept two very special items which he had kept in reserve. He had offered them to Drake for five million dollars each.

Drake needed both, but since Cooper had screwed up his plans with the Pilgrim girl, he had only nine million stashed inside the Cessna. And Kudinov wasn't going to like that. Not at all. The items he would be bringing with him to this meeting in Key West were a pair—a set of twins, so to speak—and he wanted to unload them both together, and forever. Just being in possession of them was dangerous both legally and physically. And Kudinov wanted them gone.

As the Cessna taxied toward the refueling area just off the tarmac, Drake unbuckled his seat belt, stood up and walked to one of the overhead storage compartments. He reached to the back and pushed on a small, uneven scratched spot in the bottom left-hand corner. The scratch looked as if it had been caused by the hard, sharp corner of a piece of luggage carelessly thrown into the compartment. But it hadn't. It had been scraped into the plastic with a screwdriver to mark the spot that, when pressed, caused a hidden panel to swing out from deeper inside the plane.

And that panel swung out now.

Over the years, Harry Drake and his men had used this hidden compartment to smuggle everything from drugs to weapons. They had done business from the top of Canada to the tip of Argentina. But those days were about over. At least Harry Drake hoped they were. If things went well, Kudinov would probably sell him one of the backpacks he'd be bringing to the meeting, and take the other four million as a down payment on the other.

Drake would have to find some other way to get the last million he needed. But he had an idea in the back of his mind that should easily suffice.

The secret compartment popped open, and Harry Drake pulled two soft-sided, expandable suitcases from the opening. Setting them briefly on the deck of the Cessna between the seats, he felt the other men's eyes on him as he replaced the false back panel and then closed the overhead compartment again. Then, lifting one case in each hand, he walked down the aisle past Whitlow, Bundy, O'Hara, Scott and Ducket, and dropped down out of the plane.

He had felt the other men's eyes on his back as he passed, and it had made him feel uneasy. Several of his men had begun giving him strange looks every time he took his pills and downed a shot of whiskey. Others had expressed a desire to just divide up the nine million dollars they already had and go their separate ways. It had taken every bit of persuasion Drake could muster to convince them to follow through with their business with Kudinov. After they put into operation Drake's final plan, they would have a *billion* dollars to split among themselves.

There were several uniformed police officers and two customs officials in the area as Drake lugged the heavy suitcases, one in each hand, toward the terminal. One by one, they all glanced his way, then turned their backs. Drake had to fight off a smile. If he hadn't greased so many palms down here in Key West over the years, he'd probably have the extra million bucks right now. But convincing the proper authorities that all he smuggled were pre-Columbian artifacts from Central and South America, and the occasional load of marijuana—big deal—had been money well worth handing out. Truth be told, Drake knew that he'd have no cash at all, and be sitting in some federal penitentiary right now, if he hadn't invested so much money in gratuities.

Drake walked to the first cab he saw on the other side of the terminal and got into the backseat, waving the driver away when he tried to take the suitcases and stow them in the trunk.

Instead, he pushed them both into the back of the cab and then slid in next to them.

Harry Drake gave the cabdriver an address, then sat back to think as the vehicle took off. He watched through the open back window as they drove by the U.S. naval station, a sponge pier and a turtle crawl. The smell of fish grew stronger in his nostrils and soon they were passing the fish market. Eventually, they reached the address downtown that Drake had given his cabdriver.

Refusing to allow the cabbie to touch his suitcases again, Drake dropped them at his feet as he got out of the backseat. He reached into his pocket and pulled out a small roll of bills, handing the driver enough to cover the trip and adding a medium-size tip. The tip was as carefully calculated as every other part of Harry Drake's plan. Enough to not draw attention to himself as a skinflint, but not so much as to make him memorable as a high roller, either.

Drake picked up the suitcases and turned toward the address he had given the driver. It was a small, European-style café with outside tables that sat beneath umbrellas advertising various alcoholic beverages. Slowly, he squinted against the sun and surveyed the people sitting in wrought-iron chairs.

The man he was looking for was easy to find. He sat facing the sidewalk with a small glass and a bottle of Russian vodka on the table in front of him. He was broad shouldered, brown bearded, and wore what Drake immediately recognized as a Spetsnaz undershirt. Blue-and-white horizontal stripes crossed his chest, and the garment's deep boatneck provided a glimpse of the well-developed muscles beneath the stripes.

Alexi Kudinov held up his shot glass in greeting.

Drake smiled back. The Spetsnaz T-shirts had been available at Army surplus stores all over the U.S. ever since the cold war had ended. And they looked right at home in a casual beach atmosphere like Key West.

Drake lugged the suitcases through an open gate in the iron fence surrounding the sidewalk café, and walked to Kudinov's table. The Russian had pulled a chair out for him by the time he arrived. Carefully sliding the suitcases beneath the table where he could keep track of them with his feet, Drake sat down.

Before they could begin speaking, a young, beautifully bronzed blond waitress arrived wearing nothing but a bikini and high heels. Drake looked her up and down, then ordered a beer. A moment later, he stared at the swing of her hips as she strutted back inside the café.

"So, you have arrived safely and you have brought me something," Kudinov said, breaking the ice. He turned to his side in the chair and reached down, lifting two medium-size nylon backpacks with one muscled forearm. "And as you can see, I have something for you, as well."

Drake nodded. He started to speak, then, just before the first word could leave his mouth, he suddenly realized that he was about to go into his Iranian accent. That was an aspect of this mission that had been designed simply to throw American authorities off his trail, and of which Kudinov knew nothing. It would only confuse the Russian and, besides, Kudinov had no need to know about it.

Clearing his throat, Drake said, "I've got most of what I promised you. Had a little problem, however."

The Russian's bushy eyebrows lowered. The dark brown orbs set deep in his weathered skin stared holes through Drake.

Leaning slightly in, Drake said, "I'm a little short. One of my fund-raising campaigns—" even though they were speaking in generalities, he took a quick glance around to make sure no one was listening "—didn't work out."

Kudinov put both elbows on the table, then leaned in on them. "How short are you?" he asked.

Drake glanced around again. Before he could answer, the Russian said, "Stop looking about like that—you are only drawing attention to us that way. The only other people who are paying any attention to us are my men. And they are watching from far away. Through rifle scopes."

A shot of anxiety pierced Drake's chest. He thought of the pills he had in the pocket of his slacks but decided not to take them in front of the Russian. A second later, the stroke of fear had gone, anyway. He nodded, more to himself than Kudinov. The Russian was only taking a precaution he should have expected. Relaxing again, the former Green Beret said, "One. One million."

"Then you have nine million?" Kudinov said, glancing under the table at the suitcases Drake had brought.

Drake nodded.

"Nine is not ten," the Russian simply said. "And our agreement was ten."

"I know," Drake said. "But like I said, we had a problem. How about I give you the nine and promise you the rest in two weeks?"

"I had planned for our paths to never cross again after this day," Kudinov almost growled in a low voice. "Now, it seems that, one way or another, they must."

"You know I'm good for the other million," Drake whispered.

"I know no such thing," Kudinov said. "I do not trust you, Mr. Drake. You are far too much like me for me to trust you."

"Then I'll buy one of the packs from you now for five," Drake said. "And I'll get back with you for the other as soon as I've got the rest of the money."

Kudinov shook his head. "*Nyet,*" he said, shaking his head. "You will buy *one* backpack for the nine million you have with you. I will keep the second pack for now." The smile that now covered his face could be described by no other words than pure evil. "But look on the bright side. The second pack will cost you only one million when you buy it later."

Slowly, Drake nodded. It was what he had suspected the Russian would demand.

"And if I do not see you again," Kudinov said, "I will sell the second backpack to someone else at a reduced price. Probably someone who will use it on your fellow Americans."

Drake didn't reply. He simply stood up and took the backpack as Kudinov lifted it from the ground and pushed it across the table toward him. Leaving the two suitcases where they were with the Russian's second pack, he had started to turn away when the bikini-clad blonde appeared through the doors with his beer on a small tray.

Drake reached into his pocket, dropped a ten-dollar bill on the table, then said, "Have a beer on me, Alexi." Turning, he walked back out through the gate in the iron fence and stopped at the curb.

As he waited for a cab to come along, Harry Drake thought back on Kudinov's last words—his threat to sell the other backpack to someone who would use it on Americans. The Russian could have had no idea how little that meant to a man like Drake.

It was against his own fellow Americans that Harry Drake himself planned to use the small nuclear bombs in the backpacks.

THE EXECUTIONER CARRIED Sarah Ann Pilgrim in his arms until he reached the dirt road next to the cotton field. When he set her down, he held on to her for a moment, not trusting her wobbling legs. The poor girl had just faced one of the most horrifying deaths imaginable, and her nerves were still frazzled. It would be a while before she was herself again.

"How are you feeling?" Bolan asked.

"Like I just woke up from a nightmare," Sarah Ann said, answering Bolan's question. "I'm not sure what's real and what's not. I mean, didn't some guys who'd kidnapped me just throw me out of an airplane?"

"Yes," Bolan replied, "they did."

"And you flew down out of nowhere and saved me?"

"No, I fell, not flew. I was in another plane, following the one you were in."

Sarah Ann shut her eyes tightly for a moment, then opened them again and looked up at the Executioner. "How in the world did you do it?"

"It's not as impossible as it sounds," the Executioner said. "As soon as I'd caught up to you, I opened the parachute I was wearing and then we both floated down." He looked at her and smiled again. "Although *float* might not be the best word for the way we landed. We were so low when we opened that we hit pretty hard."

Sarah Ann Pilgrim shook her head back and forth in disbelief. "I'll settle for the way we landed," she said. "At least I'm alive."

Suddenly, the young woman reached up, threw her arms around him and cried out, "Thank you!"

Bolan held her while she cried away most of the anxiety still ingrained in her chest.

Exactly how he'd get to that landing strip, he didn't yet know.

Bolan was about to call Grimaldi when he heard the two Pratt & Whitney turbofan engines far in the distance. He looked up to see another tiny speck in the sky and held up a hand in recognition as Grimaldi dipped low over their heads when the Lear passed by.

"That means he's seen us," Bolan told Sarah Ann. "And the way it looks, he's trying to find a place where he can land."

"Out here?" the young woman asked incredulously. "Where?"

"I don't know where," the Executioner said. "But I know my pilot, and he can do things with an airplane that don't seem humanly possible."

As if he'd heard Bolan's very words, Grimaldi banked the Learjet into a wide turn back toward them. Then, dropping the rest of the way through the sky, he set the wheels down on the dirt road a little over a mile in the distance. Bolan watched as the Learjet bounced over the uneven road, occasionally disappearing for a second or two behind a hill, then rising slightly back into the air as it came up off a steep embankment.

A minute later, Jack Grimaldi brought the Learjet to a halt ten yards in front of where Bolan and Sarah stood. Cracking open his door, the pilot leaned out slightly and called to them. "Somebody here order a pizza?"

Bolan chuckled as he escorted Sarah Ann Pilgrim to the Learjet.

But Grimaldi wasn't finished with his humor. "Sorry I couldn't get any closer," the pilot said.

His words brought a giggle from Sarah Ann's lips.

A few seconds later, the Executioner and senator's daughter

had joined Grimaldi, Jessup, Wilkerson, Dunbar and Sampson on the Learjet. Sarah Ann took a seat next to the DEA agent and buckled herself in. "I'm not sure I ever want to fly again," she said, her eyes glued to Bolan in the seat ahead of her and across the aisle. "But I guess I'm going to have to." She reached forward, grabbed the Executioner's hand and shut her eyes tightly as Grimaldi took off from the dirt road.

It seemed as if they had been in the air for only minutes when Grimaldi set the Learjet down again in Charlotte. Bolan reached into his pocket and pulled out a roll of hundred-dollar bills. Handing a stack of them to Dunbar, he said, "Burt, I appreciate your coming along. But I need you to take Sarah Ann inside now, and get both of you a flight back to Atlanta. Call her parents' house and tell them you have her as soon as you get inside." He paused for a moment, thinking. He doubted that his next order was necessary, but there was always the chance that the men in the Cessna had seen him dive out after Sarah and catch her before she hit the ground. And he didn't yet know who they were, let alone how many there were and if some of them might have been in another plane and tracking them from a distance.

So there was no sense in taking chances. "And just to be safe," Bolan said, "make that call from the airport police station. And call the local FBI office. They may even want to fly her home in their own private plane."

But before Sarah Ann left, Bolan had a few questions for the young woman. "Before you get out, Sarah Ann, what can you tell me about the men in the plane?"

"They spoke a foreign language that sounded like Arabic or something," Sarah Ann answered. "But that was only when there were other people around. The rest of the time, they spoke English with American accents. But when that one guy talked to you on the radio, he spoke English with that same foreign accent."

Bolan nodded. He resisted telling her that the fact that they let down their guard like that with her around made it certain that they'd intended to kill her, one way or another, right from the start.

But Sarah Ann Pilgrim was no dummy. "That was when I *really* got scared," she said. "When they started speaking English and didn't even bother to keep their faces covered around me, I pretty much knew I was marked for death."

"Well, it's all over now," Bolan said. He got out of the Learjet and helped Sarah Ann down from the aircraft behind him. She hugged him tightly, and Bolan smiled back at her, then turned and got back up into the Learjet as Dunbar walked the young lady toward the Charlotte airport's terminal.

The Executioner buckled his seat belt again. "Let's get this thing back into the air," he told his pilot. "And not that I'm complaining, but why did you come back for us instead of following the Cessna?" Bolan was almost certain he knew the answer but he wanted it confirmed.

"I wasn't sure it was the girl who'd been thrown out of the plane," Grimaldi said. "So I was afraid to shoot it down." He turned to Bolan. Their eyes locked for a second, then the pilot's eyes flickered toward the seats behind him and the Executioner.

That was the real answer to what Bolan had just asked. While DEA Agent Rick Jessup had proved himself to be a more than adequate warrior, he was the only one on board who had. Wilkerson was primarily a paper pusher; John Sampson had been with the 101st Airborne during the Vietnam War, but that had been decades before; and Dunbar was just simply too old to count on without seeing him in action first.

The bottom line was that Grimaldi hadn't trusted the rest of the men to take down the Cessna without the Executioner leading them.

Bolan nodded his understanding and then both men faced forward as the Learjet began its takeoff again.

It had been a good decision on Grimaldi's part. True, they had lost the closest lead they'd had on these bogus Iranian terrorists, but they would pick them up again soon enough.

Moe, and the rest of his men with the phony accents, needed money for something and that meant more exposure.

And the next time they exposed themselves, the Executioner intended to be there.

HARRY DRAKE LEANED FORWARD as the Cessna took off from the Key West runway, rummaging through the briefcase at his feet for his pills and whiskey. Unscrewing the cap on the pill bottle brought a sharp twinge of pain to Drake's right wrist. It was hardly unbearable, but it was enough to remind him that he wasn't getting any younger. Simple arthritis, the doctor had told him. Happened to almost everyone sooner or later. To Drake, however, it meant old age. He knew the arthritis would get worse instead of better, and show up in more joints as he continued to grow older. The thought made him angry, and he washed down a double dose of pills with a big swig of whiskey.

"Best go easy, Harry," Joe Knox said from behind the Cessna's controls. "We'd all hate being vaporized when you set things up."

Without turning his face, Drake said, "Speaking of setting things up, up yours," he said. "I'm going to take a little nap now. Wake me before we reach Nassau. And tell those sons of bitches in the back to keep their voices down." The last sentence was spoken louder than the others, and Drake looked over his shoulder to make sure that Whitlow, Bundy, O'Hara, Scott and Ducket had all heard him. The mercenaries nodded their understanding.

Drake nodded back, then turned back to face the windshield as the Cessna rose into the air.

The next thing he knew, Knox was shaking him awake by the shoulder. "Rise and shine, old chap," the Briton said. "Nassau in five."

Drake opened his eyes. The pain in his wrist had disappeared and with it had gone the nerves that had been tingling inside his chest ever since he'd found out that this Cooper bastard had substituted old magazines for the million bucks he was supposed to deliver. Only one of his men—Tom Yancy, another former Special Forces soldier—had been on the ground to retrieve the money. They'd pick him up on their way back north after Drake did what he intended to do in the Bahamas.

Knox spoke on the radio, getting clearance to land at the airport in Nassau, and a few minutes later the Cessna's wheels were hitting the tarmac. Drake stared out the window as Knox pulled the plane into the refueling area. He sat quietly, watching the workmen come and go about their business, and watching the Bahamian customs and other officials studiously ignore the Cessna.

Drake had spread enough money around this airport to be as safe from inspection as he was in Key West. Again, he considered it money well spent.

So Drake was slightly surprised when one of the customs men—a tall, slender black man wearing a white shirt with a silver badge and a pith helmet—walked toward the American plane, carrying a clipboard. If Drake remembered correctly, the man's name was Jonathon Pinder. On his collar were the silver bars of a lieutenant.

Pinder stopped just outside the Cessna as it was being refueled and lifted his hand, motioning for Drake to open his window. When the glass barrier had been removed, the black man stuck his wrist through the opening and shook hands with Drake.

"Ah, my good friend Harry," Jonathon Pinder said. He took in a deep breath and glanced toward the sun. "It is a hot one, eh?"

"It is indeed, Jonathon," Drake said. He now knew why Pinder had come his way, and he stepped into the role he was expected to play by saying, "It's so hot a man needs a drink."

"A drink?" Pinder said as if it was the furthest thing from his mind. "Ah, yes, what a good idea."

Drake reached back into his briefcase and pulled the flask out.

Pinder stuck his head inside the plane to keep from being seen while he took two quick swigs. Then he smacked his lips together, returned the flask to Drake's hand and pulled his head back out of the craft.

But Drake knew that the whiskey was not the only reason Pinder had stopped by the Cessna, and he reached into his pocket as the customs man waited patiently outside. Pulling out a roll of hundred-dollar bills, the former Green Beret counted off five. "Have another drink on me."

Pinder's hand snaked back into the Cessna and then disappeared just as quickly into his pocket—before anyone who might be watching could have time to distinguish what was in his hand. "I will, my friend," he said. "I will." He paused for a moment, then lifted his clipboard slightly. "Do you want documentation that you were here?" he asked in a low whisper.

Drake paused for a moment, thinking. Sometimes in the past it had been beneficial that he be able to document his location here—far away from some crime he and his men had just committed. And this, he decided, was one of those times. "If you would, please, Jonathan," he said. "But it would be helpful if the books read that we refueled a couple of hours ago instead of now."

"That can be arranged," Pinder said, but now his smile became a mock-serious frown. "Of course such things are always very risky...." His voice trailed off.

"I'll make it worth your risk when we pay for the fuel," Drake said a little more bluntly than he'd intended. Sometimes he couldn't help it, though. Corrupt officials were like leeches. They'd bleed you to death if you weren't careful. Not that it would matter much longer to him, of course. He was getting out of the smuggling business for good. So he didn't intend to let a few extra dollars leave him open to the chance of getting caught. At least not on some technicality like not being able to prove he was far away from where he had been supposed to take possession of the money for Sarah Ann Pilgrim. Nor did he intend to spend the rest of his life looking over his shoulder and wondering when some self-righteous prick like Cooper would catch up to him.

Harry Drake intended to relax. He planned to buy a beach house somewhere in the Caribbean or the South of France and spend the rest of his life drinking whiskey and popping Xanax and Lortabs. Someplace where he could hire a couple of good-looking young female housekeepers who'd clean more than just his house. Someplace where he could grow fat and lazy, turn his liver into one gigantic nonfunctioning blob of fat and then die.

AS SOON AS THE REFUELING WAS complete Drake dug into his pocket for more money and handed it to Knox. The pilot jumped down out of the plane, stretched for a moment with his arms over his head, then jogged toward Pinder, who waited in the refueling area. "Mr. Pinder, sir," Drake heard him say in his British accent. "Could you take care of our fuel bill for us?" Knox handed more money to the customs man and Pinder smiled widely. He waved back at the Cessna, nodded, then turned back around and walked off.

As Knox jogged back to the plane, Drake knew that this was one fuel bill that was never going to be paid. Trying to balance the books on fuel sales this night was going to drive some poor Bahamian accountant crazy.

A few minutes later they were back in the air. And an hour and a half later, they had flown a circuitous route in order to spot any other plane that might be trying to follow them. The procedure brought the memory of Cooper's Learjet back to Drake's mind, and his brow furrowed as he wondered, for the hundredth time, why the Lear had suddenly quit following them earlier. Was it running out of fuel? Maybe. But that didn't seem likely considering how professionally methodical it had been in every other way. Engine trouble? Again, maybe. But that was a stretch, too.

Finally, the uninhabited and practically uncharted little island between Mayaguana and Caicos appeared in the distance. Knox set the wheels down on the rough landing strip that had been cleared by Drake and his men, and bounced to a halt.

When the pilot had finally killed the engine, Drake stood up and walked back to the same hidden compartment behind the overhead luggage rack that had held his briefcases before they'd landed at Key West. Pushing on the scratch in the corner, the panel popped open to reveal the backpack containing the small nuclear bomb he had purchased from Kudinov.

"Get out, stretch your legs, have a beer, but stay out of my way," Drake told the other men as he pulled the backpack down

Get FREE BOOKS and a FREE GIFT when you play the...

LAS VEGAS

GAME

7 7

Just scratch off the gold box with a coin. Then check below to see the gifts you get!

YES! I have scratched off the gold box. Please send me my **2 FREE BOOKS** and **FREE GIFT** for which I qualify. I understand that I am under no obligation to purchase any books as explained on the back of this card.

366 ADL EVMJ　　　　　　　　　　　　　　　**166 ADL EVMU**
(GE-LV-09)

FIRST NAME　　　　　　　　　　　LAST NAME

ADDRESS

APT.#　　　　　　　　CITY

STATE/PROV.　　　　ZIP/POSTAL CODE

7	7	7	Worth TWO FREE BOOKS plus a FREE Gift!
🍒	🍒	🍒	Worth TWO FREE BOOKS!
🔔	🔔	♣	TRY AGAIN!

Offer limited to one per household and not valid to current subscribers of Gold Eagle® books. All orders subject to approval. Please allow 4 to 6 weeks for delivery.

BUSINESS REPLY MAIL
FIRST-CLASS MAIL   PERMIT NO. 717   BUFFALO, NY

POSTAGE WILL BE PAID BY ADDRESSEE

GOLD EAGLE READER SERVICE
3010 WALDEN AVE
PO BOX 1867
BUFFALO NY 14240-9952

NO POSTAGE
NECESSARY
IF MAILED
IN THE
UNITED STATES

and slid his arms into the straps. "I should be about a half hour, then we'll get out of this godforsaken hellhole."

Without waiting for a reaction to his words, Drake shuffled back up the aisle to the door and exited the aircraft. Whitlow came off the Cessna next. "Want me to come with you, Harry?" Drake's former Special Forces corporal asked.

"Yeah, why not," Drake said as he shifted the pack slightly and snapped the belt around his waist. He wasn't really in the mood for company, but he liked Whitlow better than the rest of the men. He supposed that had to do with the man's longer history with him, and the fact that they had gone on so many legitimate, sanctioned missions when they'd been stationed in the Middle East.

The thick jungle began immediately off the man-made landing strip, and Drake led the way, pushing back limbs and leaves and wishing he'd had the foresight to bring along one of the machetes they'd used to clear the landing strip. The big jungle blades were still on the plane. But they were already into the midst of things, and it didn't seem important enough to go back and start over. Besides, he had no need to go too deeply into the thick foliage. Just far enough to get the nuke out of sight.

Sweat began to gather on Drake's forehead as he moved on. This island was just one of hundreds of similar tiny pieces of land sticking up out of the Caribbean, and the chances of anyone even finding it were a thousand to one. Hiding the nuke in the jungle, however shallowly, increased their odds to ten thousand to one and was simply good insurance.

When he had fought his way a hundred yards or so through the thick growth of leaves and vines, Drake stopped next to a tall palm tree. Dropping to one knee, he unzipped the backpack and pulled out the small nuclear bomb.

Drake smiled now, remembering how he had protested when SOCOM had decided to send him to what was called nuke school. He'd seen no sense in it back in those days, and the prediction that the U.S. Special Forces might someday come across such devices, and need men who knew how to disarm them, had seemed preposterous to him.

Now, Drake knew as he wiped the sweat from his face and slapped at a mosquito with the other hand, it was about to prove to be the most lucrative training he had ever had. Because in order to know how to defuse a nuke, you first had to learn how to arm one.

The entire process took only a few seconds. As soon as the bomb had been activated, Drake connected it to a wireless router, whose frequency was then programmed into a remote-control device that looked little different than a TV channel changer. But looks were deceiving, and this remote had the capability of penetrating the thick jungle foliage that surrounded the bomb after bouncing off a satellite. The only drawback that Drake could see was that it had a one-hour delay time during which a counter code could be entered to disarm the device.

Even the Soviets, Drake knew, realized that mistakes could be made and they needed a backup cancellation plan.

When he was finished, Drake stood back up. "Let's get out of here," he said to Whitlow.

Whitlow led the way back, following their path through the jungle. He stopped and waited for Drake to catch up as soon as he reached the cleared landing strip.

Just as Drake stepped out of the jungle, Whitlow cleared his throat and said, "Heaven forbid, Sergeant, that anything should happen to you before we collect our money and all go our separate ways. But just in case, don't you think I should know the code you programmed into the remote, too?"

If it had been any of the other men, Drake would have probably told him to go screw himself. But he trusted Whitlow, and the man's words did make sense. "Yeah," he said. "You should know. But don't worry. It's an easy one to remember."

"And what is it, Sergeant?" Whitlow asked.

Drake stopped, slapped at a mosquito on his arm and wiped more sweat from his face. Then he smiled and said, "Why, it's 9-1-1, Corporal. What else would it be?"

Whitlow let out a low grunt of laughter. "Quite appropriate,

Sarge," he said. "And I can't imagine I'd need this, either, but the disarming code you spoke of earlier on the plane?"

"It's 419," Drake said. "That's 4-19—April 19."

"The Oklahoma City bombing," Whitlow said, nodding. "Another good choice."

"Yeah," Drake said. "But if they force us to detonate the second nuke in the States, it's going to make both of those incidents look like grade-school fistfights." He pulled a bandanna from the back pocket of his fatigue pants and wiped his forehead. "You got it?" he said. "And we'll use the same codes on the second bomb, once I've picked it up from Kudinov. Or maybe I'll send you to get it. Personally, I'm getting a little sick of that Russian asshole."

"For my share of a billion bucks, I can put up with quite a bit of asshole behavior, Sarge." Whitlow grinned.

6

"They were still heading south when I turned around, Striker," Jack Grimaldi said as the Learjet reached cruising altitude. "Of course that doesn't mean they kept going in that direction." Stony Man Farm's number-one pilot took off his suede bush pilot's cap, ran the sleeve of his weathered leather jacket across his forehead, then put the cap back on his head.

"But it doesn't mean they didn't, either," Bolan said from the copilot's seat. He reached forward and pulled the radio mike from its hook on the control panel. As with the other Stony Man communications gear, the Learjet's radio was fitted with scramblers and the signal bounced off at least two satellites before a call reached its destination and became unscrambled.

"So which way you want me to go?" Grimaldi asked as the Executioner keyed the microphone.

Bolan nodded his head forward, telling the pilot to just keep cruising for the time being. Then he said into the mike, "Striker to Stony Base. Striker to Stony Base. Come in, Base."

"Stony Base here, Striker," Barbara Price, the Farm's mission controller, replied. "Come in."

"Hook me into Bear, will you?" Bolan came back.

A moment later, Aaron Kurtzman's voice came over the airwaves. "I'm here, big guy," the man in the wheelchair said.

Bolan looked across the control panel and read the instruments in front of Grimaldi. "Our current coordinates are 33 degrees north, 78 west," he said, "and we're continuing south."

Bolan's gut told him that the kidnappers had kept heading south. They could not have missed seeing the Learjet give up the chase and turn back. Which, in turn, meant they'd have had no reason to change from the next step in their original plan.

Whatever that next step might be.

"Coordinates entered, Striker," Kurtzman said. "Now, what can I do for you?"

"Calculate the distance a Cessna 550 Citation II can fly before it has to be refilled."

Bolan felt eyes on the side of his face and turned to see Grimaldi frowning at him. "There are a lot of variables," the pilot whispered.

Bolan let up on the microphone's red button and said, "I know, Jack. Hang with me. I'm about to turn this over to you in a minute anyway."

Grimaldi shrugged and turned back to the front of the Lear.

"You know what kind of engines the Citation has?" Kurtzman asked over the screeching and scratching radio.

Bolan handed the mike to Grimaldi. "Twin 11.12 kN, 2500 lb st Pratt & Whitney Canadas, Bear," the ace pilot said.

Bolan opened the small glove box in front of him and pulled out a map of the United States and a ballpoint pen. He had opened it on his lap, then refolded it to show the Eastern Seaboard.

"JT15D-4B turbofans," Grimaldi added.

"Okay," the man in the wheelchair said. "That information's entered. Now what?"

Bolan had drawn an X on the map to represent their current location. He leaned over and let Grimaldi hold the mike in front of his face. "Now, subtract a quarter of a tank of gas. That's guesswork on my part. But I've got to figure they used up that much fuel before reaching the drop spot."

A few seconds later, Kurtzman said, "Done."

"Great," the Executioner said. "The only problem we have now is whether or not they continued south or switched courses after you left them, Jack."

"I wish I could tell you, Striker," the pilot said. "But—"

Bolan shook his head back and forth. "I'm not blaming you," he said. "You did what you had to do under the circumstances, with the information you had at the time." He took the mike back from Grimaldi, then said, "Subtract another half tank of fuel so that we're down to a quarter tank, Bear," he said into the instrument.

More tapping. "Done, Striker."

"You have a map in front of you?" Bolan asked the wheelchair-bound computer genius.

"I can pull one up…there."

"All right," Bolan continued. "Now, assuming they're going to start thinking about refueling when they get down to a quarter tank, give me some towns heading south—probably in Florida—where they might have stopped."

A half minute went by while Kurtzman's fingers went back to tapping the keyboards. Then, after another ten seconds of silence, Kurtzman said, "They'd have been well past Jacksonville when they hit the one-quarter mark. Somewhere between Orlando and Fort Pierce, probably. So they could easily have made it on down into the Keys. Key Largo or Key West would be the most likely spots."

"What makes you say that, Bear?" Bolan asked. Even if it was only a hunch, the Executioner trusted Kurtzman's instincts almost as much as he did his own.

"Well," the man in the wheelchair said, "they want to get as far from you as they can, as fast as they can. I mean, that's why you figured they probably kept to the southern route, isn't it?"

Bolan couldn't help but smile. The Bear had a genius-level IQ and common sense to match. "That was at least part of it," he told the man.

"Okay, there are a lot of landing areas where they could refuel before the Keys," Kurtzman went on. "But they're all small airports. They'd be remembered. I'm guessing they wanted a place large enough to blend in with the crowd." A short cough, then a clearing of the throat came over the speaker. Then Kurtzman went on with, "And we both know there are hundreds of private aircraft flying down that way every day."

"So which is your best guess?" Bolan asked. "Largo or West?"

"Key West," Kurtzman said almost immediately.

"You sound sure of yourself."

"I am."

"Care to tell me why?"

"Because they wanted you to think they were veering off to the southwest," Kurtzman came back. "When they're really heading farther southeast."

"And how did your computers come up with all this?" the Executioner asked, frowning.

"I just hacked into the refueling records in the Bahamas," Kurtzman said. "They topped off what they'd used since Key West in Nassau."

Bolan's frown turned into a smile. "What do you do in your spare time?" he asked the man in the wheelchair.

"Play chess against all of my computers at once," Kurtzman quipped.

"Who wins?"

"I do."

"Always?"

"Almost always."

"I'm not surprised," Bolan said. "We're heading toward Nassau, then."

"According to the books, they refueled over two hours ago, then flew out again."

"That's impossible," the Executioner said. "Unless, of course, you've got somebody in Nassau on your payroll."

"That'd be my guess," Kurtzman said. "You need anything else out of a broken-down old bruin like me?"

"Not at the moment," Bolan said. "But I'll probably get back to you before this is all over."

"Anytime, Striker," Kurtzman said.

Bolan let up on the radio button and rehung the mike in its slot. He turned to Grimaldi. "You heard the man," he said.

Grimaldi nodded, then dipped the left wing slightly and turned the plane toward Nassau.

SAL WHITLOW LOOKED at the small backpack nuke on the jungle floor as Drake finished setting it up and connecting it to the router. He was glad Drake was doing all of this because even the word *nuke* scared the living hell out of him. Granted, this was a small one as nukes went—just large enough to make this uncharted island and maybe a couple of the other nearby pieces of land sticking up out of the Caribbean go up in a mushroom cloud and then sink into the sea like the fabled Atlantis. And standing next to Drake was as dangerous as doing the work himself. If anything went wrong, they'd both be vaporized— as would the rest of the men back at the makeshift landing strip—and never know what hit them.

But it was a responsibility Whitlow still didn't want, and he was happy it had been his former Green Beret sergeant rather than him who'd been sent to nuke school back when they'd still been part of the Army.

Drake finished, stood up, and they both looked down at the device, so mechanical and out-of-place amid the thick jungle foliage. "Let's get out of here," he said.

Halfway back to the plane, Whitlow watched as Drake stopped, pulled a canteen from his web belt and took a long drink. He offered the canteen to Whitlow, but the former corporal shook his head. He knew the canteen contained not water but whiskey, and he didn't know how Drake could stand it in this heat. He had taken to mixing the alcohol with pain pills and some other kind or downers, as well.

The corporal only hoped the substances Drake was putting in his system didn't take over before his former noncom could complete his final few steps in this mission. It was Drake, and Drake alone, who had the contact in the White House who could convince the President to pay the extortion demand of a billion dollars. After that, Drake could chug a gallon of whiskey and overdose on all the pills he wanted to as far as Whitlow was concerned.

Whitlow had always liked Drake. At one time, the man had been one of the best of the best. But considering the substance abuse during the past few months, Harry Drake had become the very definition of a loose cannon.

A cannon that might explode in Whitlow's and the other men's faces at any given moment.

Finally, as they reached the edge of the foliage and stepped out into the light, the former army corporal saw the azure waters of the Caribbean lapping softly against the shore less than twenty feet away. He took a good look, and knew it was probably the last good look any human being would ever take at this particular shoreline.

In less than twenty-four hours, the gentle tide coming in would turn to gigantic tidal waves that would travel far across the sea, probably destroying many similar islands as surely as any hurricane. Then he looked back to Drake, who was taking another pill with another sip from his canteen. Yes, Sal Whitlow thought sadly, Harry Drake had once been both his friend and commanding noncommissioned officer. He was still his friend.

Which was just going to make it all that much harder to kill the man when his usefulness was over.

At the end of the landing strip, Whitlow saw that Joe Knox had turned the Cessna around so they could take off again. The other men—Bundy, O'Hara, Scott and Ducket—were all sitting next to the water, drinking Jamaican Red Stripe beers and passing around a quart bottle of rum. That was okay. They all knew when to stop before the alcohol began to affect their performance.

Drake didn't. And for that, he would have to die. Whitlow had talked it over with the rest of the men in private, and they agreed. If the unthinkable happened and Drake was captured, he'd give up his White House contact, the rest of his team and their entire plan for a single drink.

And they certainly couldn't afford taking a chance that would happen.

Joe Knox revved the Cessna's engine, telling the rest of the men that he was ready and that they should make their way down to the plane. They all stood up in almost military unison, leaving their beer bottles and the rum on the ground where they had been sitting.

"Pick up that litter!" Drake suddenly screamed at the top of his lungs. "You assholes want someone to see that and blow all of our plans?"

Bundy, O'Hara, Scott and Ducket exchanged quick glances. The chances of anyone seeing a few beer bottles on the coast of this remote island were even less than anyone noticing the landing strip. And the chances of anyone seeing them and concluding a primed nuclear bomb was hidden nearby were too remote to even calculate. It was yet another indication of Drake's fragile mental state. But they reached down and gathered up their trash just the same. Better right now to play along with Drake's delusions. Soon they would never have to put up with him again.

Whitlow joined the group as they walked toward the Cessna. The next step was to somehow come up with the extra million dollars they needed for the second nuke. And only Drake could deal with the mysterious Russian after that. Then it would be Drake's duty to contact his friend in the White House via an unpublished e-mail address with the threat to wipe out New York, Los Angeles or some other major American city. None of them expected the man in the Oval Office to just cough up a billion dollars, even with the evidence that the extortionists obviously had knowledge of the secret e-mail address.

But the explosion of a nuke in the Bahamas would be considerably more convincing.

Once Drake had done the things which only he could do, the rest of the men had all agreed he was a liability.

As they reached the Cessna and began to board, Whitlow's lips were pressed slightly together. There was one final step in this operation of which only he was aware. And that was that after the billion dollars had been secured, as many of the men as possible—Bundy, O'Hara, Scott, Ducket and Yancy—would be dispensable, too.

If six men and their children and grandchildren could live like kings on a billion dollars, then one man and his descendants could live like gods.

And Sal Whitlow intended to be that man.

BOLAN UNBUCKLED HIS SEAT BELT, stood up and walked down the aisle between the seats. Rick Jessup's eyes were closed and he snored softly. The DEA special agent had obviously taken the Executioner's advice to sleep whenever the opportunity presented itself once a mission had begun.

John Sampson was reading one of the paperback novels Grimaldi kept on board for times when he had nothing to do but wait for the Executioner, and Wilkerson stared straight at Bolan as he passed, as if every tiny movement of the Executioner's body might present a threat to the United States of America.

Skirting the round table and chairs, Bolan moved to the last locker along the wall and lifted the latch, listening to the bolt screech through the hole in the locking device, then swing open. Inside the locker, on the top shelf, he saw a neatly stacked pile of passports.

Bolan, of course, had his own U.S. passport identifying him as Matt Cooper, as well as access to others from a variety of countries. Grimaldi was equally covered, and Jessup could use his real passport, since it said nothing about his association with the Drug Enforcement Administration.

As to Sampson and Wilkerson, Bolan didn't know.

Returning to the passenger area, the Executioner rested his arms on the back of an empty chair at the rear of the aisle. "Sampson?" he said, and the white-haired man turned toward him. "You and Wilkerson have your passports with you?"

Sampson nodded.

Wilkerson shook his but said, "I don't need one. If I heard you right on the radio, we're heading into the Bahamas. I've been there before. My FBI credentials will get me in."

Bolan fought the temptation to close his eyes and sigh at the man's narrow outlook on the world. He had seen it before in the paper pushers who always seemed to find their way up the back stairs to promotion after promotion in both the armed forces and police work.

Instead of snapping back at the FBI agent, the Executioner said, "That's exactly what I want to avoid. I don't want any of us, or this plane, associated with law enforcement in any way, shape or form." He paused long enough to wave the FBI man back toward him. "Come with me for a second," he said.

Wilkerson unbuckled his belt and followed the Executioner back to the lockers.

Bolan began going through the stacks of passports, opening them to the pictures and trying to find one that bore at least a passing resemblance to Wilkerson. Finally, he came across a picture of a man who might pass as Wilkerson's little brother if he'd grown a beard and had longer hair. He glanced up at the FBI man, then back down to the passport.

It was nearing expiration date and showed an issue date of almost ten years previously. It should work. Men's looks changed a lot over the years of their lives, and it would appear to anyone who looked at the picture that Wilkerson—who would now go under the name of Bruce Roberts—had shaved, gotten a haircut and added a few wrinkles to his face.

Bolan handed the document to the FBI agent. "Here you go, Bruce," he said.

"Bruce?" Wilkerson echoed.

"Bruce Roberts. That's your name until we get back on U.S. soil. Now, give me your FBI badge and credentials."

"What?" Wilkerson said. "No way I'm—"

"I can take them from you if I have to," Bolan said. "But that's going to hurt and make you walk kind of funny for a while. So why don't you just willingly give them to me and do like you've been ordered."

Slowly and reluctantly, Wilkerson reached into the inside pocket of his pinstriped suit and pulled out his credential case. Then he unclipped the badge from his belt and handed both forms of identification to the Executioner.

Bolan stuffed them into the locker on top of the rest of the passports. "Just be glad I'm letting you keep your gun," he said. He was about to close the door when he heard a voice behind him. "Cooper?"

The Executioner turned to see Jessup standing next to the table. The man held his DEA badge and credential case in his hands, too.

"Saw what just happened," Jessup said. "You better take these, too."

Bolan nodded and tossed them in on top of Wilkerson's IDs. He had intended to let Jessup keep his papers, knowing the DEA agent was sharp enough not to go flashing them around once he caught on to what they were about to do. Wilkerson, on the other hand, would have stepped off the Learjet with his badge shoved into everyone's faces.

When they had returned to their seats and buckled themselves in again, Bolan turned to Grimaldi. "How far out are we?"

"Ten minutes, maybe," Grimaldi said. Then his voice lowered to a whisper. "I called in for clearance while you were back there taking that poor little boy's candy and toys away from him." The pilot shook his head. "Naughty, naughty. That guy probably doesn't even know who he is now."

Bolan let a small grin cover his face. Grimaldi was closer to the truth than most people would have realized. There were men in this world—especially in law enforcement and even more especially at the federal level—whose very identity was dependent upon their guns and badges.

Nine minutes later, Jack Grimaldi was setting the Learjet down on a runway reserved for privately owned aircraft.

Bolan turned in his seat and said, "Jessup, I need you to come with me. You, too, Sampson."

Wilkerson was already beginning to rise up out of his seat. Bolan couldn't afford to let that happen. "No, Wilkerson," he said, shaking his head. "Somebody needs to stay here and help my pilot guard the plane. He can't do that, get refueled and supervise a maintenance check at the same time."

The FBI man stared at the Executioner, knowing that what he'd heard were simply excuses.

And he was right. Even with his identification secreted away, Wilkerson might as well have had FBI stenciled on his forehead. No way he could pass as a criminal. He was just too stuffy.

A tall black man carrying a clipboard walked across the tarmac toward them as Bolan, Jessup and Sampson dropped down out of the plane. He wore blue slacks with a red stripe running down the outer sides of the legs, a white pith helmet and silver badge that reflected the bright Bahamian sun almost blindingly.

"Just follow my lead," the Executioner whispered to Jessup and Sampson. "And, John, pay careful attention to everyone's voice we talk to. See if anyone seems out of place."

Both the linguistics expert and the DEA agent nodded their understanding.

Bolan led the way to meet the customs officer roughly halfway between the plane and the small building that housed the paperwork for the private planes. Behind him, he heard Grimaldi taxi the Learjet away toward the fuel pumps.

"Good day, gentlemen," said the man in the pith helmet.

"And good day to you, sir," Bolan said, smiling. He handed the man his Cooper passport. After the customs officer had given it a cursory look, he handed it back. "And may I ask what your trip here concerns?"

"Just came down for the day," Bolan said. "Had a run of luck at a casino in Atlanta last night and my friends and I decided to just blow it all at once. There's a little place in downtown Nassau, a café, I can't remember its name but—"

"Gladwyn's," said the customs man.

"That's it." Bolan nodded, smiling. "Best seafood in the Caribbean."

"At least that's what he's been talking about for the last three hours," Jessup said with a bored yawn. "We'll find out, I guess."

Bolan had been carefully studying the customs man ever since they'd shaken hands. And his instincts now told him the man could be bought. He'd have to be careful. But it was worth a try.

Reaching into his pocket, the Executioner pulled out the huge roll of hundred-dollar bills. "Tell me, er—"

"Jonathon," the customs man said, his eyes flying immediately toward the money. "My name is Jonathon."

"Tell me, Jonathon," the Executioner said. "Is this where we pay our landing fee?"

"You can if you like," Jonathon said, his smile widening.

Bolan slid three hundred-dollar bills off the top of the roll and handed them to the customs man. "That should cover it, I think," he said.

"Oh, indeed it does," Jonathon told him. "Of course there is the inspection fee—"

Another three hundred insured that there would be no inspection of any kind.

"One more thing I'd like to ask you, Jonathon," the Executioner said. He was still holding the big roll of cash in his hand but was careful to keep it between him and the customs agent so no other curious eyes around the airport could see. "Where does a man get information around here?"

"There is an information desk in the main terminal," said the customs man, then waited for the next question. A slight change in the set of his brown eyes told the Executioner he was taking the right track.

"I don't think they'd have the kind of information I'm looking for," Bolan said. "It's more of a...*personal* nature."

"Well, then," Jonathon said, a huge smile spreading across his face, "perhaps I can help."

"I bet you can," the Executioner said. "We were supposed to meet some friends in another plane down here. They should have arrived before us. But I don't see them."

Jonathon frowned. "What were their names?" he asked.

"Well," Bolan said, laughing slightly and looking down at his feet. "That's the funny—and kind of embarrassing— part," he said. "I can't remember their names. We all got pretty drunk at the casino in Atlanta last night, and got to know these guys, and they said they had their own plane and they'd meet us here."

"Do you know what kind of plane they have?" Jonathon asked.

John Sampson stepped in slightly. "Didn't that one guy—the taller one—didn't he say it was a Cessna?" he asked Bolan.

The Executioner turned slightly his way. The man was proving to be not only an expert in linguistics, but a good undercover intelligence actor, as well.

Jessup, of course, had had years of undercover experience. So Bolan was far less surprised when he picked up on the cue and said, "Yeah, I'm sure it was a Cessna, they said. Citation II, I believe." He laughed. "Unless all of those olives they kept putting in my martinis damaged my brain."

Bolan watched as Jonathon's bright eyes turned suspicious. "The only Cessna that has landed came in much earlier today," he said. "And they refueled, then flew out again." He pulled a page up and over the clip on his clipboard, then nodded. "Yes. It was much earlier. Almost six hours according to my records here."

The Executioner knew the man was lying. And had been paid well to do so. Lifting the money roll slightly in his hand, he peeled off ten hundred-dollar bills and stuck the rest back in his pocket.

The customs man's eyes watched greedily as each hundred came off the roll.

"Let's quit playing games," the Executioner said in a soft voice. "Here's a thousand bucks to tell us the truth."

"You are…American police of some kind?" Jonathon asked.

"Not exactly," Bolan said. "But it's important that we meet with these guys and do so fast. Now, do you want the thousand or not?"

Jonathon's eyes revealed his thoughts again and he nodded, suddenly assuming that Bolan, Sampson and Jessup were criminal associates of the men in the Cessna. He took a quick look around, then snatched the hundred-dollar bills from Bolan's hand and stuck them in his right front pocket. "You must promise not to let them know where you obtained this information," he almost whispered. "They are good—how should I put it—customers of mine. Repeat customers. You understand?"

"I understand," the Executioner said. "Now tell us the truth."

"You missed them by less than an hour," Jonathon said. "The rest of what I told you is true. They refueled, then left again. Their destination is anyone's guess."

The Executioner stepped forward and turned at Jonathon's side, looking down at the clipboard.

Jonathon pointed at the third line from the bottom. "There, you see?" he said. "The plane is registered to a man named David Macy."

"You looked at the paperwork?" Bolan asked. "Saw the actual title?"

"No," Jonathon said. "It was simply a name I made up." Neither the tone of his voice nor his facial expression betrayed any feelings of guilt at his dishonesty.

A plane on a nearby runway took off and Bolan had to wait until it had passed over their heads to be heard again. "Anything else you can tell us?" he asked.

The customs man glanced down at the Executioner's pants pocket. "I wish there was," he said. "They were all dressed in green fatigues as if they might be heading out toward one of the more remote islands or at least heading for the jungle somewhere."

"That's worth another C-note," Bolan said, pulling a single bill out of his pocket and handing it over. "They didn't file a flight plan?"

"No," Jonathon answered.

Bolan nodded. "I've changed my mind," he said. "I don't think we'll be going downtown to Gladwyn's after all." He turned and started back toward the fuel pumps in the distance.

Jonathon cleared his throat, then said, "Sir? What name shall I say this plane is registered to?"

"Give it to Dave Macy, too," Bolan said over his shoulder and kept walking.

Jessup and Sampson followed Bolan to the spot where fuel was still being pumped into the Learjet, and all three men climbed aboard. Wilkerson turned his face toward the window, sulking, as they resumed their seats.

The four men sat in silence until the tanks were full again, and Bolan watched Grimaldi pay for the fuel, then open the pilot's-side door and climb up behind the controls. "Find out anything?" he asked Bolan as he buckled himself in.

The Executioner shook his head. "They were here roughly an hour ago, refueled like we did, then flew out again."

"And my guess is they didn't file a flight plan," Grimaldi said as he warmed the Learjet up again.

"Good guess," Bolan said.

"So…" Grimaldi said. "Where to?"

The Executioner was about to tell his pilot to head back toward the States when Barbara Price's voice came over the radio. "Stony Base to Flyboy One. Stony to Flyboy. Come in, Jack."

Grimaldi grabbed the mike as he taxied the Learjet away from the pump toward the runway. "I'm here, Barb," he said.

"Is Striker still with you?" Price asked.

Grimaldi sighed dramatically as he handed the mike over to the Executioner. "Always the bridesmaid," he said. "Never the bride."

Bolan chuckled as he took the mike. "I'm here, Barb," he said. "What's up?"

There was a long pause, then Price keyed the base microphone once more. "Hal needs to talk to you ASAP," she said.

"Know what it's about?" Bolan asked. The conversation and mood had suddenly turned serious.

Deadly serious.

"He just got a call from the President," Price said.

"Concerning?" Bolan asked.

"An e-mail came to the White House threatening to detonate a nuke in a major U.S. city unless the sending party received a billion dollars."

Bolan frowned. "They get those kind of threats every day, Barb," he said. "Over the phone, through e-mail, snail mail, every which way. The Secret Service checks them out, and they're almost always from nut jobs who didn't get enough attention from their parents when they were kids."

"This one's different, Striker," Price said.

"How so?"

"It came in on a top-secret e-mail address used only in-house. At the White House."

The Executioner felt the sudden rush of adrenaline start in his chest and descend into his abdomen. Suddenly, he knew what it was that these fake Iranian terrorists were trying to raise enough money to buy.

And that they'd finally gotten that money. Or were at least close enough to put their nationwide extortion plan in motion.

"Affirmative, Barb," Bolan said. "Tell Hal we're on our way in. Striker out."

"Stony Base out."

Without needing to be told, Grimaldi played with the controls in front of him, setting course for a direct flight to the Farm.

"Put her in high gear, Jack," Bolan said. He turned to see what reaction the transmission had had on the men seated behind him.

John Sampson was holding two black hoods, and using one to show Wilkerson how the drawstring worked.

Rick Jessup already had his hood on.

7

Harry Drake reached beneath the seat and pulled out the quart bottle of whiskey. Out of the corner of his eye, he saw Joe Knox glance his way, then look back to the front.

The pilot had a slight frown on his face.

Piss on him, Drake thought. All the men had noticed that he was drinking more and taking more pills as they neared the climax of this mission, and what would undoubtedly be the high point in each and every one of their lives. Drake didn't care what they thought. He held the bottle between his legs as he fished in the breast pocket of his BDU blouse and came up with his pill bottle. He had mixed the Lortabs and Xanax together rather than carrying them separately, and now he popped a pair of each into his mouth.

Drake felt the rough surface of the pills with his tongue, and noted the bitter taste he had grown to expect—and love—as he unscrewed the cap from the whiskey bottle.

It took two swigs to get the four pills down. But Drake took a third just for good measure.

Recapping the bottle, he replaced it beneath his seat and settled back to allow the drug-and-alcohol mixture to take effect. With his eyes closed, he pictured Whitlow, seated directly behind him. Even his former Green Beret corporal had begun looking concerned whenever the pills and the whiskey came out. But he needn't be. And he shouldn't be, for that matter. Back when they'd still been in the Army, he and Whitlow and the rest of their SF team had subsisted on nothing but water, grub worms and speed tablets for weeks in the

jungles and deserts of the world. Whitlow knew him, and knew
him well. Which meant he knew that in addition to all of his
other responsibilities, Harry Drake could handle any drugs he
dumped into his system.

"I assume we're still goin' in the right direction, aye, Harry?"
Joe Knox said, breaking the silence in the front of the Cessna.

Drake opened his eyes yet again. The alcohol and other
drugs had kicked in and suddenly he felt on top of the world.
Unfortunately, he knew this feeling of euphoria wouldn't last
very long. Oh, he'd feel okay for another couple of hours. But
it wouldn't be this good for more than ten minutes or so.

"If you're angling toward Tennessee, you're still on course,"
Drake said and was slightly surprised when he heard himself
slur the words. Not bad. Just a little. He glanced down at his
watch. No matter. He'd be stone-cold sober by the time they
reached Memphis.

Drake had enjoyed giving Knox only the vague order to
"fly northwest" when they'd left the uninhabited island in the
Bahamas. It reminded the pilot, as well as all of the others, just
who was in charge of this deal. He was. Harry Drake. And he
could give out what information he wanted to give out, and
withhold what he didn't want them to know yet. Drake glanced
at his wrist again. But there was no need to keep their destination a secret any longer. So he said, "We're gonna land in
Memphis," then shut his eyes again to concentrate on the elation
coursing through his veins.

The former Green Beret felt his lips curl into a slight grin.
He had kept this next job a secret just in case they ran into any
money trouble like they had with the Sarah Ann Pilgrim
ransom. None of the rest of the men—not even Whitlow—had
any idea where they were going. In fact, they didn't even know
who Marlin Morgan was.

The name meant nothing to them. They didn't know that
Marlin Morgan lived in a house almost as big as Elvis's
Memphis mansion, had inherited so much money that he'd
never had to work a day in his life and, along with priceless

works of art and other expensive items, kept stacks of hundred-dollar bills hidden in a safe in his elaborate bedroom.

The rest of his crew didn't know anything about Marlin Morgan because they hadn't grown up with him as Drake had. They hadn't gone to school with him or attended any of the wild and raucous parties Morgan had thrown at the house their senior year in high school after his parents had both been killed in a car wreck. Drugs and alcohol had flown about the grounds like raging rivers, and more Memphis teenagers had probably lost their virginity at Morgan's mansion than any other site in Tennessee.

Drake smiled, thinking about his old friend. Morgan had a hell of a cocaine problem now. But he was too rich to ever hit bottom. He was one of the few cokeheads whose investments stayed ahead of his habit, no matter how much of the white powder went up his nose. And Marlin Morgan was an Elvis freak himself. Half of the rooms in the mansion were decorated with Elvis memorabilia and at this very moment, Drake knew, old Marlin would be all dressed up in one of his sequined jumpsuits just like the King himself had worn when he made his comeback in the early 1970s. He hadn't seen Morgan in a good ten years, but he'd wager all he owned that the man was still wearing that stupid black wig and the big metal sunglasses, too.

Drake wondered if his old friend was still snorting his cocaine or had finally given in and turned to the needle. Not that it mattered. He was just curious.

The important thing to know, however, was that there'd be far more than the million dollars they still needed packed into that wall safe in the upstairs bedroom. And all they'd have to do was take out a half-dozen security guards, then turn off the alarm system.

That part would be a joke. Two former Army Special Forces men, two Navy SEALs and a pair of Marine recons against six rent-a-cops.

It would be like taking candy from a baby.

Drake felt himself frowning. He had forgotten something. What was it?

Oh, yeah. The Doberman pinschers. Morgan had several of them trained as attack dogs and they roamed the fenced-in estate looking for anything they could eat, including human beings they didn't recognize. That was an important thing to remember. But that was why each of the men had added a sound-suppressed Ruger .22 automatic pistol to his personal arsenal. They were going to do their best to keep even one shot from being fired that could alert the neighbors. True, the nearest neighbors were probably half a mile from the house, but Drake wanted to take no chances now that they were this close.

If all went well, both the security guards and the dogs would die with .22 Long Rifle rounds in their brains. After they forced Morgan to open the safe, they'd take the money and be gone in less than fifteen minutes.

Of course they'd have to kill Marlin Morgan, too, but he and Drake had never been *that* close. At least not a billion dollars' worth.

Drake knew he had drifted off to sleep when he felt Joe Knox's hand shaking his shoulder. "Wake up, Harry," the pilot said. "We're here."

The former Green Beret looked out the window and saw that night had fallen. They were taxiing off a runway toward an area where several other small business-class airplanes were parked in a row. He had called ahead on his cell phone and rented a large Lincoln Town Car using a credit card he'd taken from the last bank job, and he could see the vehicle waiting a short distance from the planes. Unbuckling his seat belt, he turned to see that the rest of the men had already wrapped their weapons up in blankets or other nonlethal disguises, and stacked them next to the Cessna's side door.

"Whitlow," Drake said, yawning as Knox pulled the Cessna to a halt, "go back the car up as close as you can to the door. The keys are supposed to be in the ignition."

"Gotcha, Sarge," Whitlow said and slid the door open far enough to jump out.

Drake watched him sprint to the Lincoln, wondering if he

and the men should have changed out of their BDUs to civvies for this job. So far, it hadn't mattered. Like in all of the other strikes, they simply looked like reserves or National Guardsmen to a nation that had grown used to seeing far more OD fatigues around since September 11, 2001.

A moment later, the Lincoln was backed up. Whitlow popped the trunk and the former Marines and SEALs dropped the blanket-covered weapons into the opening before slamming the lid closed.

"Knox," Drake said to his pilot, "you stay here as always and deal with the paperwork."

Knox nodded as Drake dropped down out of the Cessna and walked to the shotgun door of the Lincoln.

A few seconds later, they were leaving the Memphis airport and were on their way toward Morgan's mansion.

DUSK HAD FALLEN over Stony Man Farm when the Learjet's wheels hit the runway. One of the Farm's regular blacksuits was waiting in a black Hummer to take Bolan and the rest of his crew to the main house. Bolan and Grimaldi helped the hooded men into the vehicle, then in through the front door. Not until Bolan had punched the digital code into the lock on the door of the War Room itself did the hoods come off.

"Boy," Jessup said, "you guys really trust us, don't you?"

"It's not that," Bolan said, shaking his head. "It's just that if word ever does leak out about this place, we don't have to waste valuable time eliminating you as suspects this way."

"I was kidding." Jessup smiled.

"I wasn't," Bolan said. He heard a buzz, reached down and twisted the knob, then pushed the door open and held it as all of the rest of the men except Grimaldi filed past him.

"Unless you need me for something, Striker," Stony Man's top pilot said, "I've got a couple of adjustments I want made on the bird."

"Take off." The Executioner nodded as the last man— Sampson—filed past him.

Bolan stepped into the War Room and stopped. Even before his eyes confirmed the fact, he sensed that there was a big difference here since his last visit. The first change he noticed was that Hal Brognola was not at his usual place at the head of the long conference table. Instead, Stony Man Farm's director of sensitive operations had taken a seat to the right. He was standing in front of his chair, and had to twist to see Bolan as he entered the room.

Two new faces had been added to those around the table. One was familiar, the other not. The face Bolan had never seen before belonged to a mousy-looking little woman in her early to midforties. She was dressed in a conservative navy-blue suit over a white blouse buttoned all the way up to the throat. Her dark blond hair had been pulled back into a tight ponytail, and her arms were tightly crossed over her chest.

The other face belonged to the President of the United States. He was standing in front of the chair at the head of the table where Brognola usually sat.

Bolan walked toward the Man, his hand outstretched. "Sir," he said.

"Striker," the President said, offering his hand.

The Executioner gripped the President's fingers in his, then let go again. Turning, he took the chair that had been left open for him just to Brognola's side. The unfamiliar woman sat just to the President's left, looking nervously down at the table in front of her.

The men all sat down together.

Bolan turned toward Brognola. "I half expected to see Able Team and Phoenix Force here to help," he said.

Brognola shook his head. "Able Team's tied up in a dope deal on the Canadian border with North Dakota," he said. "Phoenix Force is in Hong Kong. But if you need help, we've got plenty of blacksuits we can send with you."

"I'll keep it in mind," the Executioner said. The blacksuits were highly trained warriors themselves, but they weren't Phoenix Force or Able Team. The men who made up those two counterterrorist crews were the best of the best.

The President cleared his throat and all eyes turned toward him. "So tell me, Striker," he said. "What's your take on this situation?"

"Sir," Bolan said, "what we've got here is a group of five to seven men. They've done their best to cover their tracks by speaking Farsi and pretending to be Islamic terrorists, and according to witnesses at every crime scene they worked with military precision. In fact, those exact words were used to describe their actions by several people. So, military precision suggests military training, either here or abroad. In any case, they've been robbing banks, kidnapping people and committing other crimes in order to amass as much money as possible."

"Isn't that what all criminals do?" the President asked. "Try to get all of the money they can?" The frown on his face indicated that he wasn't being sarcastic. But he was not a trained investigator or soldier, either.

"Yes, sir," Bolan said. "Excluding purely unadulterated political or religious terrorists from the picture, as much money as they can get is what all criminals are after. But these men are different. And I don't just mean their masquerade as Islamic extremists."

"How so?" the Man wanted to know.

"They aren't taking any time to *spend* any of their ill-gotten gains. Common criminals are fairly predictable. They rob a bank or make some other big score, then live high on the hog until the money's gone, or almost gone. Then they go back to work until they hit another big score." He paused long enough to let his words sink in, then went on. "These guys are different. They're like schoolboys who aren't going out to the playground for recess. Which has indicated to me all along that they were working toward some final, massive operation that would set them up for life." He paused again, then continued, "I suspected it included the purchase of some sort of weapon of mass destruction. Now, after the e-mail you received at the White House, we know what kind of WMD we're talking about. Nuclear."

"God help us," the President said, looking at the ceiling of the War Room. Lowering his eyes back to Bolan again, he said,

"Could this be some rogue element of the Iranian or old Iraqi armies?" he asked. "What with the Farsi and all?"

"It's possible but highly unlikely," Bolan answered. "The Iraqis speak Arabic."

The President continued to frown. "Couldn't they learn—?"

John Sampson spoke up for the first time. "Sorry to interrupt you, sir," he said. "John Sampson's the name."

Too far away from each other to shake hands, the two men nodded at each other instead.

"Middle-Eastern linguistics is sort of a specialty of mine," Sampson said. "And I've heard enough to know that these men, while they're speaking fluent Farsi, aren't from anywhere near the Middle East. They're most likely Americans. Possibly Canadian, or even British, some of them. But I'd put my money on Americans."

"And by what means did you determine that?" the President asked.

"I felt it," Sampson said confidently. "Right here." He pounded a fist lightly against his chest.

The President turned, frowning even deeper as he looked at the Executioner for corroboration.

Bolan nodded his head. "You can believe him," he told the Man. "Call it instinct or whatever you like, but some of us have it. And he's one of us."

The President shrugged, not understanding but readily taking Bolan's word at face value.

The Executioner took the break in the dialogue to speak up again.

"Mr. President," he said. "I'll be happy to go on with this debriefing, but I'd feel a lot more comfortable about it if you'd introduce us to this lady first. And assure us that she has top-secret clearance."

"Lucille Brady is one of my finest personal aides," the Man said, briefly smiling at the petite blond woman. "And it was her in-house-only, encrypted e-mail address that someone was able to hack into and use to deliver the threat about the nuke." He reached into his jacket and pulled out a sheet of computer paper folded into thirds, which he slid down the table to the Executioner.

Bolan opened it up. It was a hard copy of the same e-mail he'd been informed about by Price as they left the Bahamas that afternoon. It had come from an address reading moneynow!@juno.com and been sent to LMBrady1401@whitehouse1112.com.

Bolan kept his eyes on the page as he said, "I'm sure your Secret Service men tried to trace this 'moneynow' address."

"They did," the President confirmed. "But by the time our boys had a fixed position, they were long gone. Our guess is they're going to use the same system they used with the cell phones. Change laptops and e-mail addresses each time they contact us, and stay on the move." He crossed his arms, then leaned forward and rested his elbows on the table. "But let me ask you this—how do we know they even *have* one of these nuclear weapons?"

"We don't know for certain," Bolan said. "But the feeling Mr. Sampson had about these men being Americans?" He hooked a thumb at his own chest. "I've got the same feeling about this. But I don't think they have one nuke. I think they either have, or shortly will have, at least *two* of them."

"Why two?" the Man said.

"Because they'll need one to detonate in some remote location just to prove to you that they can do it," Bolan said.

"Do you have any idea where, or when, it'll happen?" the President asked.

"The *when* will come when you either don't answer them back or deny their request," the Executioner said. "As to the *where,* my guess would be somewhere on one of the uninhabited islands in the Bahamas."

"And on what do you base that theory?" the President asked.

"Because they gassed up in Nassau earlier today," Bolan said. "We missed them by less than an hour. They filed no flight plan, but the most likely scenario is that they flew on to one of the remote islands and planted their nuke there."

The President's eyebrows lowered. "We can have the CIA check satellite pictures," he said.

The Executioner nodded. "It's worth a try," he said, "but there are going to be hundreds of small aircraft flying all over the Bahamian chain. Still, the boys at Langley are good. They might be able to pick out the right Cessna in time for us to get down there and disarm it before it goes off." This meeting was going on longer than he'd hoped it would. He was a man of action, and he didn't like sitting around talking when there was work to be done. "But even if we do find it and deactivate it, the result will be the same."

"What do you mean?" the President asked.

"They'll have proved they have access to small nuclear devices and can blow up a city if you don't give them their billion dollars." Bolan stared into the President's eyes. "Like I said, my hunch is that the nuke is hidden on one of the small uninhabited Bahamian islands. It'll blow that little piece of land to kingdom come if they set it off. But the only damage it's likely to do to humans would come from the tidal waves it causes. And by the time they reach populated land, they should have died down to the point where they aren't much bigger than what you'd get from an average hurricane. And the people who live in those areas are prepared for such disasters."

"What are you trying to say?" the President queried.

The Executioner paused before continuing. "The bottom line is this. I don't think anybody's going to die if that first nuke goes up. But if the thousand-to-one long shot comes through, and the satellites can pinpoint which of the hundreds of islands the Cessna landed on, I'd like your permission to go down there and deactivate the mechanism myself. Alone."

"Why's that?"

"Because the most likely thing to happen is that the bomb will go off while it's being deactivated. And I don't feel like wasting anyone else's life for something I don't personally believe needs to be done in the first place."

The President sat back in his chair. "I think we've got to at least *try* to defuse this thing if we can find it," he said, looking around the table but letting his eyes finally stop on Bolan. "And I can't let you go alone, Striker."

"Sir, there's no reason—"

"Yes, Striker, there *is* a reason. You're an expert in a lot of fields. But nuclear physics isn't one of them. Depending upon how sophisticated this nuclear rig is, you could easily find yourself standing there, looking at it and not knowing how to disarm it."

Bolan didn't like what he had just heard, but he saw the logic in it. "Then who will I be taking with me?" he asked the President.

The Man started to speak but Bolan now interrupted him. "Please don't tell me I'm not going at all," the Executioner said. "Because somebody has got to watch the back of whoever is disarming the bomb. There's always a chance that the enemy left men to guard the bomb until the last few minutes."

The President closed his mouth, letting everyone in the room know that he had indeed been about to tell the Executioner that he was too valuable a commodity to risk losing. Instead, he said, "I'll contact the CIA at Langley from here and have them start looking over the satellite shots." He pulled a satellite phone similar to Bolan's own cellular instrument out of his coat and pressed it on. "And while they're looking, I'll have them come up with the best nuke man the U.S. has in its employment."

"Be sure he knows how to use a parachute," Bolan said. "We're going to be dropping in rather than landing. No reason to waste a perfectly good pilot and airplane, either."

The President nodded and began tapping numbers into the phone.

"In the meantime, we need to stall in every way we can while we run down some other leads," Bolan told the group.

As the President stood up and walked to the corner of the room where his words wouldn't get in the way of the rest of the discussion, Bolan turned his attention toward Lucille Brady.

"Ms. Brady," he said softly. "Who knows about this secret LMBrady address besides you and the President?"

The timid, plain-looking woman looked up for the first time, meeting Bolan's gaze for a moment, then glancing away just as quickly. "No one, sir," she said softly.

"Obviously someone does," the Executioner said.

"I should have said no one that I know of," Lucille Brady said, her words barely above a whisper.

Bolan looked to the President again. He was still in the corner, talking to someone at CIA headquarters in Langley, Virginia. But before the Executioner could ask the woman any more questions, he flipped his phone closed again and walked back to the table.

"They're searching the photos and trying to contact a Dr. Philo Hoffman," the President said.

"Ms. Brady was just telling us she didn't know anyone besides the two of you who might have had access to your secret e-mail addresses," Bolan said.

"Well, there *shouldn't* be anyone else," the Man said, patting the woman on the shoulder in a fatherly manner as he sat back down. "Ms. Brady is a little on the shy side," he said. "But I can assure you that she's the hardest-working and most competent aide I have. And I trust her implicitly."

Bolan nodded, then turned back to the only woman in the War Room. Trust was usually a marketable commodity in Washington, D.C., as well as in the capitals of the other countries of the world. Sometimes it was bought and sold. Other times, it was given away or traded. And he had been getting bad vibes from Lucille Brady ever since he'd entered the room.

The little mousy-looking woman's fidgetiness went well beyond the simple nervous reactions even innocent men and women would exhibit under similar conditions. She bore a closer look, in the Executioner's estimation.

"I hate to ask you this, Lucille," he said politely, "but for the sake of time, would you object to taking a polygraph test? We have a man right here who could administer it, and that would put you completely in the clear. Just so we don't have to waste time looking in the wrong direction."

At the mention of the word *polygraph,* Lucille's head had snapped up again, telling the Executioner all he needed to know, even without the lie-detecting instrument.

This woman—this trusted aide to the President of the United States of America—knew more than she was letting on.

Bolan had expected resistance to his suggestion from the President. But the Man had watched Lucille's reaction, too, and now he kept as quiet as the rest of the people in the War Room. An awkward silence fell around the conference table. Ten, then twenty seconds went by, with each one of those seconds bringing a deeper level of strain to the room.

Finally, the Executioner said, "Ms. Brady, did you hear my question?"

Lucille Brady looked up. "Yes, Mr. Striker, I did," she whispered, choking slightly.

Bolan spoke to her almost as gently. "Then would you answer it, please?"

Lucille Brady's lips opened to speak, but no words came out. It was as if her brain was telling her mouth what to say but the mouth refused to comply. Finally, she turned to the President and said, "Could we speak privately, sir?" It was the meekest voice she had used since the meeting began.

The President shook his head. "No, Lucille, you may not. I'm an administrator, not an investigator. But, if you like, you can speak with me and Striker alone. Would that make you feel more comfortable?"

Lucille Brady turned to Bolan.

Early in his career, Bolan had learned that different people had to be interrogated different ways. Some responded to browbeating. Others to threats, and still more to pain. But once in a while, you ran across a basically good person who, for whatever reason, had simply made a bad mistake. When they were as naturally shy as Lucille Brady, such negative reinforcements only drove them deeper within themselves, and unless you were willing to use torture—which Bolan was not—they only responded to one thing.

Kindness. A kindness that they lacked in the rest of their lives. You filled the vacuum that had usually been the catalyst for their mistake with kindness, and suddenly they were telling you their entire life story.

Lucille stared at Bolan for a second, then turned back to the President and nodded, the skin of her face suddenly flushing with blood.

"You have an empty room nearby here, Hal?" the President asked Brognola.

"Striker can show you," Brognola said. "The rest of us will wait here."

Bolan had already stood up and walked to the door. This time, he held it first for Lucille Brady and the President, then passed them in the hallway and walked to another door across the hall. Like the War Room, and almost every other room in Stony Man Farm's main house, this door had a digital combination that had to be opened before entering, and the Executioner tapped in a series of numbers, then held the door yet again as the Man and Lucille Brady walked in.

The room was a small, general-purpose office that Brognola often used when he needed to stay close to the War Room. In was Spartanly furnished with a simple wooden desk, desk chair and two small couches facing each other in front of the desk. The walls were a continuation of the maps and monitor screens in the larger room they'd just left, as well as containing several dozen Wanted posters of terrorists and other criminals put out by the FBI.

The President had his arm around Lucille Brady's shoulders as he walked her to one of the couches. They sat down, and Bolan dropped himself on the other couch, facing them. By now, Lucille Brady was crying into a handful of tissues she had pulled out of her purse.

Both Bolan and the President waited quietly until she regained control of herself.

"I'm sorry," Lucille finally squeezed between her lips, and the words brought on another fit of sobbing. When she could speak again, she said, "I never should have done it, Mr. President. Oh, how can I ever make it up to you?"

The President was obviously out of his element—more used to arguing with senators and congressmen than consoling women who were weeping with guilt. He looked over to Bolan on the other couch, a helpless expression on his face.

Bolan leaned forward, took one of Lucille Brady's hands out of her lap and held the tiny fingers between his own hands. "I know what it's like to be lonely, Lucille," he said quietly. "I'm alone almost all of the time."

Lucille looked up and her face told the Executioner he had established the common ground he'd been searching for. They were linked together now. So he pushed on.

"He told you he loved you, didn't he?" Bolan said.

Another nod was followed by another fit of crying.

"Don't be embarrassed," the President said, finally picking up on the Executioner's approach. "We've all been hurt by love in one way or another. We've all been lied to."

Lucille was still crying as she nodded yet again.

"What reason did he give you for wanting the e-mail address?" Bolan asked.

Lucille regained her composure again and looked up. What little mascara she wore had dripped down her face and made her look like a little girl who'd gotten into her mother's makeup kit. "He said he wanted to be able to talk to me no matter where he was in the world," she said softly. "Oh, he used to write the most beautiful poems to me. Sonnets—" Suddenly, she realized again that it had all been a ruse to take advantage of her and resumed crying.

Bolan and the President sat quietly, waiting.

When she could speak again, Lucille said, "He said he wanted to marry me."

"These people are professional con men, Lucille," Bolan told her. "They'll do anything, and say anything, to get what they want. They don't care who they hurt." He paused a second, considering how to phrase his next question. Lucille Brady didn't strike him as a lady who would want revenge. But she did seem the type who would want to help and even save the lives of others.

"Lucille," the Executioner said again after a short pause, "unless we catch this man first, he and his associates are going to detonate a nuclear bomb in the middle of some major U.S. city. Tens, if not hundreds of thousands of people will die. Thousands more will be affected by the radiation, and even more in the chaos of the aftermath." He stopped speaking, hoping the magnitude of his words was sinking in. "The entire nation's economy and social structure is likely to be destroyed, Lucille. Which means we're open to attack by any and all of our enemies around the world, and believe me, we've got plenty of them." Still holding her hand with his right, the Executioner reached slowly forward with his left hand and lifted the frightened woman's chin so that she was forced to look him in the eye.

At first, she looked terrified. But then something she saw in Bolan made her relax. Finally, she nodded, and a tiny smile even played at the corners of her mouth.

"You made a mistake, Lucille," Bolan said in his gentlest of voices. "We all make mistakes. All of this is not your fault, and I'm sure the President has no intention of bringing you up on any charges if you help us now."

Bolan glanced to the President. The Man's deadpan expression told him nothing, but his words were gentle. "You didn't do anything to harm this country intentionally, Lucille. I know that. Just answer this gentleman's questions and everything will be fine."

"I...I don't know what to tell you," Lucille Brady whispered.

"First," Bolan said, "do you know the man's name?"

"Frank," Lucille said. "Frank Norton." She paused. "At least that's what he told me. I don't know what to believe now."

"Where did you meet him?" the Executioner asked next.

"At a bar in my neighborhood," Lucille said, looking down again. "Isn't that embarrassing? I must seem like a common—"

"We're not making moral judgments here," Bolan interrupted her. "We're trying to get to the truth and save people's lives. What else can you tell me?"

"Well…" Lucille closed her eyes tightly in thought. "It seemed like he drank a little bit too much. Not real drunk all of the time. Just sort of…well, consistently. Does that make sense?"

"Yes," the Executioner said. "What else?"

"He took pills, too. He said they were for his blood pressure, but he acted different when he took them."

"Where can we find him?" Bolan asked next.

Lucille shook her head. "I don't know," she said. "He told me last week that he'd be away on business for several days."

"Has he used the e-mail address to contact you since then?"

"No," said the still-frightened woman. "He's only used my White House address to contact the President with his threats. I mean, if it's really him doing all this. I can't really believe he's the kind who would—"

"Take my word for it, Lucille," the Executioner said. "He's the kind who would. He's just exceptionally good at not seeming to be the kind who would. But you said he's only used your White House address to contact the President. Can I infer that he's e-mailed you at home or some other place at another address?"

"He used to," Lucille said. "But I haven't heard from him at all since he left a few days ago."

"I assume you kept them, though?" Bolan said. "The older e-mails he sent you?"

"Yes," Lucille acknowledged. "They're still on my home computer."

"Where do you live, Ms. Brady?" Bolan asked.

"I have an apartment," Lucille said. "It's in Georgetown."

Bolan stood up. "Mr. President," he said as the Man helped Lucille to her feet, "I'd suggest you get some of your Secret Service agents to accompany Ms. Brady to her place—" He stopped, looked down at the little woman, and said, "This Frank, he's been to your place, I assume?"

Lucille's head dropped lower as she nodded. "Several times," she said.

"Anyone else visit you there?" Bolan asked. "Friends, family, anything like that?"

"No," Lucille said without looking up. "He's been my only caller since I moved into the apartment five years ago."

The Executioner could see how such a lonely woman could be tricked by someone like Frank. Turning back to the Man, he said, "Tell them to dust the whole apartment. If no one's been there but Lucille and Frank, we might get lucky and ID this Frank Norton with a print. And send the best computer geeks you can find, too. I doubt they'll be able to trace any of Frank's old e-mails but they can try." He walked to the door.

Bolan had started to reach for the doorknob when it swung away from him on its own. He looked up to see Barbara Price about to cross the threshold. The mission controller held a single page of paper in her hand.

"They told me I'd find you here," Price said, nodding behind her toward the War Room. She held the paper out to Bolan.

The Executioner took the page and glanced down at it. What he saw was a hard copy of a new e-mail from Lucille Brady's top-secret address to that of the President's.

"You've had your warning," it read. "Unless we hear from you within the next six hours we will detonate a nuclear bomb somewhere to prove that we can. This one will be relatively harmless. The next one will not."

The note hadn't been signed.

Bolan looked up from the paper to Price. "Where's Jack?" he asked.

Price glanced down at the gold watch on her slim wrist. "Should be on his way back from Washington right now. He took off to pick up Dr. Philo Hoffman. Hoffman's a nuclear specialist."

The Executioner nodded and started to walk past her, but

Price grabbed him by the arm. He had been too busy to notice before, but in her other hand the mission controller held several large still photos that appeared to have come from a surveillance satellite. "I think we got lucky," she said. "Bear hacked into the CIA files and found these."

Bolan laughed softly. "What's the CIA doing?"

"I suspect they're still looking for them," Price said.

The Executioner looked down. There were several photos of a small island taken from various distances with a telescopic lens. The latitude and longitude were stamped in the margins. One photo showed the island in relationship to the rest of the Bahamian chain. Another showed a Cessna aircraft sitting on what appeared to be a recently cut strip of flat land on the otherwise foliage-covered island. Several men were standing and sitting around the plane, smoking and drinking beer.

Another man was about to enter the jungle but had turned back for a last glance toward the plane or something around it.

Several of the men's faces were visible in this photo, and Bolan pivoted on the balls of his feet and handed the close-up photo to Lucille Brady. "Are any of these men the man who told you his name was Frank?" he asked.

Bolan watched the woman study the picture. Suddenly, she jerked as if something hot had burned her. She turned sideways and pointed down to the man about to enter the jungle. "I don't see Frank in here," she said, "but that man is a friend of his. He met us at the bar one night. I think his name was George."

Bolan walked quickly on past Price and entered the combination to open the War Room door. As quickly as possible, he ran down what he'd learned from Lucille Brady to Brognola and the rest of the men, and advised them he was about to return to the Bahamas with a nuclear specialist.

All of the other men wanted to go.

Bolan gave them a fast thumbs-down. "If something happens to me, there have to be people still able to carry on the fight," he said. "Stay here, or follow up any other leads that come up until I get back."

"I don't like quitting in the middle of a mission," Sampson complained.

"Neither do I," Jessup argued.

Wilkerson remained his usual sullen and silent self, but Bolan could see that even the by-the-book man was against staying behind.

"You aren't quitting," the Executioner said. "You're working on a different aspect of the case." Without further words, he turned and nodded to Price, Lucille Brady and the President of the United States as he passed them again in the hallway.

By the time he had exited the main house and reached the runway, Grimaldi had the Learjet ready.

8

A small, one-room guard building, constructed of stacked cinder blocks painted light tan, stood just inside the gate to the front entrance of Marlin Morgan's mansion. The rest of the twenty-acre estate on which the palacelike house sat was encircled with a ten-foot, spike-topped iron fence. Harry Drake knew from years ago when Marlin Morgan had told him about it that two electrical wires also encircled the property but were hidden within the hollow iron crossbars of the fence. The first, when turned on, contained an electrical charge. While it wasn't quite strong enough to kill a person of reasonable cardiovascular health during dry weather, it had enough juice to seriously discourage anyone who tried to climb the fence from attempting to try it again.

The second wiring system was a silent sound-and-motion detector that alerted the closest Memphis PD substation that security at the mansion was being breached.

Both systems were activated through controls in the guard shack. Morgan had never shown or told Drake exactly where, but the former Green Beret knew it wouldn't take him long to find out.

Drake directed Whitlow, behind the wheel of the rented Lincoln, to drive past the entrance, watching the men in the guardhouse through the lighted windows as they passed. A light mist had begun to fall over Memphis, and Whitlow reached up and turned the Lincoln's windshield wipers on low. Inside the small building, four of Marlin Morgan's personal security men sat around a metal desk they had converted into a poker table. Another lay on his side on a couch, thumbing through a magazine. A sixth man had his eyes turned upward to what Drake assumed was a screen of some type he couldn't see.

It might be a surveillance camera. On the other hand, it might just as easily be a rerun of *The Beverly Hillbillies.* None of the men inside the security office looked particularly competent or well trained for their work. But what bothered Drake was the fact that all six were in the guard shack together.

That was just plain stupid if his information was correct that each shift was made up of a half-dozen men. Some of them should have been out patrolling the grounds, and guarding the iron perimeter fence.

On the other hand, it might be that they were simply lazy, Drake thought. Or wanted to get out of the rain. Let's face it, he told himself. As much as Marlin Morgan might want to be Elvis Presley, he wasn't. And there probably had never been an attempted burglary in the mansion's history. That, in itself, was enough to turn unprofessional, minimum-wage security guards into lazy louts just putting in their time to collect their pathetic paychecks.

Behind him in the Lincoln, Drake heard Bundy speak up. "You think he's hired more men, Harry?" the former Navy SEAL asked. During the drive from the airport, Drake had informed the rest of his men that there were supposed to be six guards to a shift. And Bundy was obviously thinking along the same lines that he was.

"Maybe," Drake said. "I doubt it, but you never know." They were well past the gate and out of sight of the men inside the shack. "Pull over, Whitlow. And turn around."

The man who had formerly served under Drake in the Army Special Forces did as he was told without speaking.

Even in the large Lincoln, they were crowded with three in the front and three in the back. So Drake was unable to twist anything but his neck as he got ready to address the rest of the men again. He had decided to leave their rifles and regular handguns stashed in the trunk. If all went well, they wouldn't need anything but the sound-suppressed Ruger .22 Long Rifle pistols each man wore on a web belt around the tail of his BDU blouse.

"Guys," Drake said, "this is either going to be a lot easier than I thought or we're in for some surprises I hadn't counted on. My guess is that all of the guards just ducked in out of the rain. On the other hand, Bundy might be right—Morgan very well may have beefed up his security shifts. He's been drinking and doing drugs for so long now that a little paranoia in his system would seem about right."

"We going Iranian on this?" Elmer Scott asked.

Drake knew the man wanted to know if they'd be speaking Farsi instead of English, and continuing their charade as terrorists rather than mere criminals. "I don't see any need for it on this one," he said. "It's getting late in the game. And besides, I don't plan to leave anyone here who's in any shape to provide the cops with information."

The other five men chuckled, understanding exactly what that meant, and taking the fact that they were going to kill everyone at the mansion no more seriously than they would if Drake had just told them a dirty joke.

"So what do we do?" O'Hara asked from where he sat in the middle of the backseat.

"Whitlow will drive you three in the back up as close as he can to the gate without being spotted. No one saw any security cameras along the fence anywhere, did they?"

All of the men shook their heads.

"Then they won't see us stop and let you out," Drake went on. "One break we've gotten is that these guys are wearing almost the same OD BDU uniforms we are. The only thing different is we're not wearing badges or shoulder patches," he went on. "But these fatigues should still add a second or two to the real guards' response time while they try to decide if we're from their company or not, and wonder what we're doing here."

He paused, took a drink from the whiskey bottle, then dropped it on the floor at his feet. He had skipped the pills this time. But he promised himself he would double up on them later, as soon as their business at Morgan's mansion was over. "Whitlow, me and Scott will drive right up like we own the place. I want every last man in that building dead before any of them can pick up a phone or activate an alarm. That means we're going to have to bullshit our way past the gate. Meanwhile, the rest of you will be making your way through the trees. As soon as we drive through the gate, I want you double-timing it into the estate, too. We all go into the guardhouse and put very quiet .22s into these men's heads."

It was hard to read the men's faces in the darkness, but Drake tried anyway. If his vision was clear, what he mostly saw was boredom.

These men—Special Forces, Marine recons and Navy SEALs—had faced professional killers, terrorists and drug cartel hit men for most of their careers. Security guards they could take out while standing on their heads.

When he got no response, Drake said, "Let's go, then."

Whitlow threw the Lincoln in gear and drove forward. Roughly fifty yards from the driveway, he stopped again and the men in the backseat got out. Drake opened his door and got out, too, finding that even during this short drive from the Memphis airport his legs and hips had stiffened up. A combination of age and the weather, he realized, as he limped around the open door to the backseat. The life he had led had worn out his joints early, and they were particularly sensitive to changes in the barometer like this rain was producing.

Taking a seat in the back, Drake pulled his door closed and ordered Whitlow to drive on. The man behind the wheel turned into the driveway, and as the Lincoln's headlights swung past the guard shack Drake saw the men inside look up from their various time-wasting activities. Whitlow brought the front bumper of their vehicle to a halt a few inches in front of the gate. Drake exited the backseat and walked toward the iron. Far in the distance, in the illumination brought on by the Lincoln's headlights, he could see Morgan's mansion at the end of the curving driveway.

At the same time that he reached the gate, Drake saw a tall, nerdy-looking man come out of the security office wearing a bright yellow slicker over his OD uniform. Drake waited for him.

By the time the man was within speaking distance, Harry Drake's BDUs were soaked with water and more rain was sliding down the sides of the other man's yellow slicker.

Drake spoke first. "We need to come in and talk to you guys," he said without greeting the man first.

The nerd frowned. He had hunched his shoulders and pulled his neck down against the rain, as if that might keep his face dry. It didn't, and Drake had to fight to keep the smile off his face as he saw that the idiot had snapped the yellow slicker closed all the way up to his throat.

He could be killed ten times over before he got to the pistol he carried beneath the garment.

"What's this about?" the nerdy guard asked. He stared at Drake's uniform, then added, "Are you guys with National?"

Drake let out a loud, impatient breath. National had to be the name of the security company who furnished the guards for Marlin Morgan.

"What's it look like?" the former Green Beret said. "You think we wear this crap for the fun of it?" Before the man in the slicker could answer, he continued impatiently, "Open the gate and let us in. I don't want to stand here in this friggin' rain and explain everything to you, and then have to do it all over again for your men inside the building, there."

The rain had been another thing on their side, Drake realized. It only made sense to speak briskly and insist on going inside to shelter from it.

The tall, skinny man in the slicker evidently understood and agreed. He turned and waved at the guardhouse. "Open her up, Chuck!" he shouted.

Almost as if to confirm Drake's line of thinking, the rain began to fall even harder as the iron gates swung inward. Drake walked through them and headed for the guardhouse as Whitlow drove the Lincoln inside. Just as he mounted the two steps to the building, Drake heard the sound of feet pounding on the driveway and looked over his shoulder to see the rest of the men sprinting his way.

Whitlow got out of the Lincoln and put a sound-suppressed .22 Long Rifle round between the eyes of the man in the slicker.

Drake drew his own suppressed Ruger as he opened the door and stepped into the office area.

The men inside the guard office froze in place. They were unsure of what was happening and incapable of handling the situation even if they'd known what was going on.

"None of you move," Drake said as he stepped to the side of the door to allow the other five men to enter the office area. As they moved past him, and began to pull a variety of handguns out of the guards' holsters and pat them down for backups and other concealed weapons, he pointed the barrel of his Ruger out the window, toward where the man in the slicker lay. "You see what happened to your friend?" he said.

Some of the heads around the room nodded. Others were too petrified with fear to move at all.

"Then if you don't want to find yourselves in the same shape, you'll do exactly what I tell you to do," Drake said. He had the Ruger pointed toward the desk where the men had been playing cards, and he felt a slight tremble in his hand. Dammit, he thought. He should have taken the pills along with the whiskey. But there was no time for that now.

"Who's in charge here?" he demanded.

The guard who had been reading the magazine still lay on his side on the couch. Slowly, he sat up and held up his hands.

Drake noted the sergeant's stripes on his sleeve just below the shoulder patch. Closer now, he could read the patch which, as he'd suspected, said National Security.

"Show me where the alarm switches are," Drake said. "And don't try to screw with me or you'll die just like your friend. I know there's a security wire and an electric wire running completely around the property. I want them both turned off."

The man wearing the sergeant's stripes stood up, his hands in the air without having to be told. "Follow me," he said in a shaking, squeaky voice. He walked to the back of the office area and opened what appeared to be a closet door. Inside, on a small table, Drake saw a two-way radio base station. A walkie-talkie was resting in the charger next to it. But what interested him more was the breaker box mounted on the wall.

Although there was a large white sticker in the center of the breaker box, it had not been written upon. Marlin Morgan evidently expected his security staff to memorize which breakers belonged to the various electrical circuits on the grounds.

All Drake could see was that all but one of the breakers was turned on.

"That one that's already off," said the sergeant in his screechy voice. "That's the electric fence. We turn it off when it rains anyway."

"I'll let you prove that to me in a minute," Drake said, shoving the sound suppressor up under the man's chin. "What about the motion-and-sound detectors? I want both the fence and the ones connected to the house turned off, too."

Slowly, to prove that he was following orders rather than trying anything foolish, the sergeant reached up and flipped the two switches just above the one that controlled the electric fence. "There," he said, his voice still shaky. "The top one's the perimeter fence. The one below it just deactivated both the motion and sound detectors on the doors and windows of the house."

"Great," Drake said. "Now, let's see just how honest you've been." Maneuvering around behind him, the former Green Beret shoved the sound suppressor into the man's back and marched him back through the office area, down the steps and out into the rain. Directing him toward the fence, they stopped just in front of the bars.

"Now," Drake said, "reach forward and grab a bar with each hand."

The sergeant hesitated. "There's a delay mechanism," he croaked out finally. "The electricity won't actually go off for another—"

Drake brought the sound suppressor around in a backhand

strike to the sergeant's face. Even above the noise of the rain, he heard a loud crack as the man's nose broke. The sergeant fell to his knees as blood spurted from both nostrils.

"Wrong answer," Drake said. "Now grab the bars and prove to me that everything's off."

"I…can't yet," the sergeant blurted out painfully. He was holding his nose with both hands. But the blood was still shooting out around his fingers.

"There's no delay mechanism," Drake said angrily. "There's an override switch somewhere. Stand up."

The sergeant rose shakily to his feet. His hair was now drenched with water and stuck to his head in long, wet strands that looked like stripes.

"You want to show me where the override switch is?" Drake asked.

"I told you," the bleeding man almost cried. "There's a delay—"

He never got to finish his sentence. In anger, Drake shoved the Ruger into his belt, reached forward with both hands and grabbed the sergeant's shoulders. Then, twisting slightly, he shoved the man with all his strength into the fence.

Rain had collected in puddles along the fence line and it was the perfect conduit to increase the lethality of the electric fence. A loud, sickening, hissing and sizzling sound issued forth as the sergeant's back struck the iron bars. Sparks and streaks of light turned the area immediately around the man into a Fourth of July fireworks show. The sergeant shimmied and shook as if he might be dancing, and the nausea-producing smell of burning human flesh met Drake's nostrils.

Finally, the sergeant fell to his knees, then forward onto his face.

Drake didn't waste time checking for a pulse. He turned on his heels and marched back into the guardhouse office.

As soon as he'd entered, the former Green Beret saw that Whitlow and the rest of his crew had pushed the other guards up to the windows facing the fence to watch. The sight made him smile. Good old Whitlow. The man had always been loyal and true, an improviser and a leader in his own right who knew how to best supplement Drake's orders.

Proof of the effect the sergeant's death had produced in the remaining guards was written across their terrified faces.

Drake stopped just inside the doorway. Like the rest of his team, he wore a cloth OD-green ball cap with the rest of his BDUs. But the rain had been hard enough to soak through the material, and now he took the cap off and shook it out before running his fingers through his hair and replacing the hat on his head. "I take it you all saw the little fireworks show outside?" he said.

Again, some of the men were too frightened to respond at all. But the rest of the heads nodded.

"Then which one of you wants to show me where the override switch is?" Drake asked.

The hand of a man of Latino descent shot up into the air. Whitlow used his sound-suppressed Ruger to push him away from the window toward the center of the room. He turned and walked back to the same closet where the breakers had been located, then reached for a small flashlight on his black nylon gun belt.

"Be very careful what you do with that thing," Drake said, bringing the Ruger up to the man's face.

The man nodded. He pointed the flashlight toward the floor, then tapped a button to turn it on. Stepping into the closet, he directed the light downward to the wall just inside the doorway.

Several old prints of paintings, the kind you could buy in any discount store, were stacked against the wall. "Behind the pictures," the man said quietly.

"Then move the damn pictures," Drake growled.

The Latino squatted and reached forward, pulling the old pictures and frames away from the wall to reveal what looked like nothing more than an average wall double switch box.

"What do those two do?" Drake demanded.

"The top one overrides the electric fence and all the rest of the security devices throughout the grounds," said the squatting man. "The bottom switch kills all electricity. Both here, and up at the mansion."

"Kill the security devices," Drake ordered. "But leave the lights on."

The man at his feet reached forward and flipped the top switch. Nothing perceivable changed around them.

"You sure the electric fence and the motion and sound detectors are off now?" the former Green Beret sergeant asked.

The man had returned to his feet. He nodded.

"Willing to stake your life on it?"

Another nod.

"Then get your ass out there next to your Kentucky-fried sergeant and grab the fence," Drake growled. "I'll watch you from the window like everyone else." He stepped back to make room for the man to come out of the closet. "You try to take off, and I'll send my fastest runner to hunt you down and kill you like a dog. And when you come back—assuming you aren't electrocuted like your sergeant—bring him with you. Now, go!"

The guard ran to the door, jumped down off the steps and sprinted to where the security sergeant still lay in the rain. Drake walked to the window and watched as he reached forward and grabbed two of the iron bars in his fists. His head swiveled on his shoulders to look back at the guard's building, he held on for a good ten seconds more, then let go and reached down, lifting the dead sergeant in a fireman's carry and lugging him back to the office through the pounding rain.

As soon as the man had returned, Drake had him drop the corpse in the corner. Then he and his men herded the remaining five guards toward the desk and had them sit back down behind the cards and poker chips still waiting on the desktop. Whitlow pushed the Latino down on the couch where the sergeant had originally been.

"I think we've gotten all we need out of these guys, don't you, Corporal?" Drake said.

Whitlow nodded, lifted his Ruger and put a .22 between the eyes of the Latino on the couch.

A second later, the room filled with the sounds of sound-suppressed .22s ending the lives of the rest of the remaining security guards.

"Dammit," Drake said as soon as the last man had fallen from his chair at the desk. "I forgot to ask them about the dogs and whether or not there were more guards at the house or on the grounds."

Whitlow smiled. "I asked them while you were outside," he said. "There aren't any more guards, and Morgan did away with the dogs a couple of years ago. Something about one of them biting a guest and a lawsuit." He stopped speaking for a moment, then added, "I didn't ask them about other employees, though. Could be a maid, or butler, or—"

"The answer to that is easy," Drake said. "We'll just shoot anybody we see." He holstered his Ruger. "Now, let's go get some money."

He turned to Elmer Scott. "Pin one of those badges on your shirt and keep a lookout at the window," he said. "There shouldn't be anyone else show up, but there's no sense in taking chances." He walked swiftly back to the closet, pulled the walkie-talkie from the charger, and took note of the green light on the instrument that proved it had been fully charged. "If you do get any kind of traffic," he told Scott, "I want to know about it immediately."

The former Marine nodded. "Gotcha, chief," he said.

Fifteen seconds later, Harry Drake and his fellow ex-commandos were back in the Lincoln and heading toward the mansion at the end of the winding driveway. Drake was still dripping wet from the time he'd been forced to spend out in the rain, and in foul temper. No question that he was earning his share of the money on this caper. Having to stand out in the rain, and putting up with bastards like the two Marines.

Not to mention having to screw that ugly White House bitch. That had been a job in itself. Of course it had been one of the key elements to the whole plan, and had allowed him time to search her apartment when she was gone until he found evidence about her top-secret e-mail address to the President. Still, he'd have rather one of the other men had done it. One of the Marines would have been good.

But when he looked at his watch, he saw that by now the President of the United States should have had plenty of time to get his last e-mail. And, of course, the man in the White House wasn't going to cough up a billion bucks easily.

So it was time to take the next step in the process of convincing the President to pay.

Harry Drake was almost smiling when he pulled the remote control from the front leg pocket of his wet BDU pants and tapped in the numbers 9-1-1.

DR. PHILO HOFFMAN WORE a neatly trimmed mustache and Vandyke beard below his shiny bald dome of a head. He had been smart enough to know that comb-overs simply didn't fool anyone, and had let the hair still clinging stubbornly to the sides and back of his head grow straight down over his ears and the collar of his shirt.

"He looks like Shakespeare," Grimaldi had whispered to the Executioner when he'd caught his first glimpse of the nuclear physicist. And indeed, the good doctor did resemble the bard, looking completely out of place in the blacksuit the Executioner had provided him from one of the lockers on board the Learjet.

"Isn't this thing going to be awfully hot?" Hoffman asked Bolan as he finished donning the suit.

"Yes," Bolan said. "It is. But have you ever been in the jungle before?"

"Certainly not," Hoffman said. "I've never had reason to be before. And never wanted to, either. Snakes and mosquitoes and wild animals and all that."

Bolan smiled. There was something endearing about the scientist, some indefinable quality that some people just had but most didn't. "Even though the sun's gone down, you're going to be hot anyway," he said. "And believe me, you'll be glad for the protection the blacksuit gives you."

The Executioner wore his own blacksuit. He had transferred his Desert Eagle to the nylon holster on his web belt, and already slid his arms into the shoulder rig carrying his sound-suppressed Beretta 93-R. Extra magazines for the Beretta hung from the same shoulder system beneath his right arm, with pouches toting more ammo and a variety of other equipment also attached to the belt around his waist.

"You mentioned snakes and mosquitoes, Doctor," he said. "But there are a lot more things in the jungle that bite, stab, scratch and poison your skin than that. And they come in vegetable as well as animal form. Trust me on this one. The jungle is one area where I've got my own Ph.D."

Hoffman had finished suiting up while he listened to the Executioner, and now he took a seat behind Grimaldi. Bolan sat back down in his regular position, next to the pilot. "How long, Jack?" he asked.

"About ten minutes," Grimaldi said, glancing down at the control panel in front of him. "You gonna give this guy a gun?"

Bolan twisted slightly in his seat. "You want a gun, Dr. Hoffman?" he asked.

"Please," Hoffman said. "Call me Philo. I've never shot a gun before."

Bolan nodded. "I'll provide you with cover in case we aren't alone," he said.

The nuclear physicist reached down and tapped the black leather case sticking out of a small backpack at his feet. "The weapons I need are all in here, Mr....er...Striker."

"You can cut out the 'Mr.' part, too," the Executioner said. "If we're going to take the chance of being vaporized together, we ought to at least be on a first-name basis, don't you think?"

"Yes, one would certainly think so." Hoffman smiled.

Bolan turned back. He wasn't particularly worried that these fake Iranian terrorists would have anyone on the island keeping watch on the nuke. Unlike the real Islamic fanatics, these men weren't into suicide missions. What worried the Executioner, however, was the jump they were about to make.

He glanced toward Grimaldi. Stony Man Farm's flying ace had studied the satellite photos and determined that while the homemade landing strip was long enough to accommodate a Cessna, the rough and rugged runway was too short for the Learjet. Especially at night. They had considered taking another plane from the Farm, but they needed the speed which that Learjet provided to make the flight to the Bahamas as quickly as possible.

They had only a few more hours before the hidden bomb was detonated, and Bolan didn't want to waste even a minute flying slowly southward in a prop job.

The dilemma had been resolved when Brognola had informed him that Dr. Philo Hoffman had been a sport diver when he'd been a younger man. He hadn't jumped out of an airplane for nearly twenty-five years, so he had been run through a refresher course by the Executioner earlier in the flight. A static line had been rigged up to the Learjet now, too. And while Bolan would free-fall, ready to try to get to Hoffman much like he had Sarah Ann Pilgrim in case of trouble, the doctor would rely on the automatic opening system.

It was the landing that worried the Executioner. Bolan wasn't sure what he was going to do if the good doctor broke a leg or sustained some other serious injury when they attempted to land. He supposed that as long as the man was still conscious, he could carry him through the jungle until they found the nuke, then lay him down and let him go to work.

"Time for us to get into our chutes, Philo," Bolan said, breaking the silence that had fallen over the plane while he thought.

Grimaldi reached over and stopped him as the Executioner attempted to rise out of his seat. "We clear on the pickup?" he asked.

"You'll fly back to Nassau, where a slow little Beechcraft that you can land on the island is already waiting for you. You should return about the time we're finished—I'll set flares along the runway to guide you in after we establish radio contact."

Grimaldi nodded his agreement and gave Bolan a thumbs-up.

Bolan walked on to the locker area of the Learjet and lifted his packed chute, sliding it on and buckling it firmly around his waist. Then he helped Hoffman into his pack, which was then connected to the static line.

The Executioner tried to keep the smile off his face as he assisted the nuclear expert. The man looked absolutely ridiculous in the blacksuit, which was stretched taut across his pot belly but gathered in folds across his sunken chest and skinny arms. Keeping his mirth hidden was even harder when Hoffman looked up at him, tried to flex a bicep and said, "This garb *does* give one a sense of power, doesn't it?"

Bolan nodded and turned away.

Two minutes later, Grimaldi called to them over his shoulder. "Ten seconds, Striker!"

"You're going first," Bolan said as he felt the small jolt that meant Grimaldi had slowed their pace through the air. He slid the door open and the wind rushed into the aircraft. When he spoke again, he practically had to yell to be heard. "I won't jump until I see that your chute has opened."

"Go!" Grimaldi shouted, and Philo Hoffman leaped from the open doorway.

By now the Learjet was barely flying fast enough to keep from falling out of the sky. But Bolan knew that was to keep him as close to Hoffman as possible. A second later, the doctor hit the end of the static line, his chute flowered open like a charm and he began drifting downward.

Bolan yelled "Geronimo" for Grimaldi's benefit and dived through the opening.

The Executioner free-fell until he had fallen even with the nuclear physicist. When he was satisfied at the distance, he pulled the rip cord and his own parachute blossomed out above him.

The Executioner was approximately twenty yards to the side of Philo Hoffman and ten feet below. The wind was almost still, and he continued to drift straight downward toward the landing strip on the isolated island.

Bolan hit the ground first, rolling to his side and popping back up on his feet. He had already gathered his chute in halfway when Hoffman touched down. The doctor's chute fell straight down on top of him to hide him from Bolan's view.

The Executioner hurried over, pulling the Caledonian Edge folding knife from his blacksuit and flipping the blade open with his thumbnail. He lifted the edge of Hoffman's parachute and found the man tied up in the lines like a roped calf at a rodeo. A few quick slices with the razor-edged Caledonian had Philo Hoffman free again.

"Okay," Bolan said as he helped the man to his feet. "Gather up what you need out of your pack. I'm going to walk this landing strip until I see sign of where they entered the jungle."

Hoffman nodded. "I won't be long," he said, pulling the same black case Bolan had seen before from the small backpack he had worn during the jump.

Using the light of the full moon in the sky, the Executioner walked out to the edge of the water to get the widest view possible of the jungle's edge. But as soon as he'd stopped, he reached into a pocket of his blacksuit and pulled out a small penlight. The size of the flashlight was deceptive, for when he thumbed it on it sent a flood of illumination a hundred feet across at the jungle.

Bolan spotted the break in the thick foliage almost immediately. The plant life on this tiny piece of uninhabited land had grown wild and free of disturbance, and the spot where the phony Iranian terrorists had broken and trampled that free life stuck out distinctly.

Bolan turned back to where Philo Hoffman was standing, his black case hanging at the end of his arm. "This way, Philo," Bolan said, pointing the penlight to his right.

Both the Executioner and the nuclear physicist started walking toward the broken limbs and vines Bolan had spotted, meeting halfway there. The Executioner led the way, frowning slightly when he saw no marks in the disturbed vegetation that looked as if they'd come from a machete. It looked more as if the men who had hidden the nuke somewhere within this densely forested jungle had simply pushed aside what vines, leaves and other obstacles they could, and broken off by hand the vegetation they couldn't duck around. That told the Executioner two things.

First, the path to the bomb was likely to be shorter than it would have been if they'd been able to cut their way smoothly through the jungle with machetes.

And second, these criminals masquerading as Middle-Eastern terrorists were no more perfect than any other men. They made mistakes.

Like forgetting to bring their machetes.

Behind him, the Executioner could hear Hoffman huffing and puffing, trying to keep up as they stepped over and around the thick growths. Bolan ignored the insects attacking them, knowing that slapping or brushing them off wasted energy and that there were always millions more ready to take their place.

Philo Hoffman, however, slapped repeatedly at his face and neck, occasionally cutting loose with a string of profanities and vulgarities that seemed entirely out of character from the man Bolan had gotten to know on the flight from the U.S.

In certain areas of the jungle, the foliage was so thick it grew together over their heads to completely block out the moonlight. When that happened, Bolan was forced to rely completely on the penlight to lead him farther along the trail. In other spots, however, the lunar light drifted down through breaks in the branches, and the path was easy to follow.

And the Executioner soon learned that he had been right in his guess that without machetes, the bomb would have not been hidden too deeply in the jungle. A hundred yards or so into the thick foliage, he caught a glimmer of metallic reflection in the bright light of the penlight.

Bolan directed the tiny flashlight toward the shiny substance. And saw something completely out of place on an uninhabited island.

Stainless steel.

"We're here, Philo," the Executioner told the man behind him as he stopped and turned around.

But Dr. Philo Hoffman was nowhere to be seen.

"Philo! Doc?" Bolan shouted.

He received no reply.

Quickly retracing his steps through the jungle, the Executioner finally found the nuclear physicist lying on his back on the jungle floor. Both of his hands were crossed on his chest, and in the bright light of the flashlight the Executioner could see that the man's skin had turned a dull, sickly gray.

Bolan knelt next to the prostrate figure. "Philo," he said, "what's wrong?" He knew the answer even before Hoffman told him.

"My…heart," the goateed man breathed out from the ground.

A strange mixture of both compassion and anger swelled in the Executioner's chest. The anger was directed toward whoever had picked this man to come along on such a physically demanding mission. The compassion was for Philo Hoffman himself.

"Why'd they send you if you had heart problems?" the Executioner demanded.

"They…didn't know…" Hoffman choked out. "I…didn't even know…"

"You've never had this happen before?" Bolan asked.

But Philo Hoffman had closed his eyes and quit breathing.

The Executioner didn't hesitate. Pressing the palm of his left hand over his right, he centered both hands on Hoffman's chest. Pressing down five times, he stopped, tilted the nuclear expert's head slightly back to open the channel to his lungs, then pressed his mouth onto the bushy mustache and beard. The Executioner gave the man two deep breaths, then returned to pressing down on his chest.

Three consecutive rounds of this resuscitation opened both Hoffman's eyes and lungs, and got his heart beating again.

"Where are we?" he asked Bolan, his eyes darting from side to side.

Bolan hesitated answering. Philo Hoffman obviously needed medical assistance far beyond any the Executioner could provide himself. Normally, that would have meant Bolan's number-one priority would have been getting him to the nearest hospital. But this was not a normal situation. They were miles—hours—from help. And while the bomb he had just spotted through the foliage was not likely to harm anyone but them, it was a prelude to the second nuke, which would take countless lives if these terrorists were allowed to go on with their plans.

The bottom line was hard yet necessary. Considering how long it would take to get Hoffman to a hospital, he might as well have a look at the bomb first. The Executioner's next problem was with Hoffman's brain instead of his heart. After all, the man had just asked Bolan where they were. Did a man who had to ask a question like that have any business trying to disarm a nuclear bomb?

Bolan breathed a sigh of relief when Hoffman's eyes cleared again and he said, "Wait a minute. You're Striker. I'm Philo Hoffman. And we're here to disarm a nuclear weapon."

"That's right." Bolan grinned down at the man. "And I think you just suffered a minor heart attack."

"Well, that explains why my chest hurts." Hoffman grinned back. Then his face turned serious. "Didn't I hear you say you'd found it right before my heart gave out?"

Bolan nodded. "It's not far from here."

The Executioner lifted the man up over his shoulder, then turned and followed the same path he'd been on earlier. A few minutes later, he had brushed through the rest of the leaves and vines to where the small nuclear bomb sat amid the dense undergrowth.

Bolan set Hoffman gently on the ground. The nuclear expert frowned at the apparatus before him. "This isn't good," he told the Executioner.

"Does that mean our situation isn't good?" Bolan asked. "Or that the bomb is constructed well?"

"Oh," Hoffman said. "The bomb is constructed *extremely* well. It's of an old Soviet design, and was undoubtedly put together by the Russians back during the cold war. No, it's so good, in fact, that your first guess was the right one. Our situation is quite dire. There are about twenty thousand ways to disarm a bomb like this. But 19,999 of them will have been rewired into booby traps. They'll blow up immediately if I try the wrong one."

"Well, what have you done in the past when you came across things like this?" the Executioner asked.

"Very, very carefully taken them to a remote spot on the planet and detonated them." He paused a second, his breathing still labored. "A place very much like this."

"So what you're saying, then," the Executioner said, "is that the best thing we can do is go back and just let this thing blow itself up when the time comes."

"That would be my suggestion," Hoffman said.

"Anything else you can try?" he asked.

"Not under the time constraints we're under."

"What time constraints?" Bolan asked. He had not run down the rest of the mission to Hoffman. The man had no idea about the e-mails to the White House.

"This device has already been activated," Hoffman said. "It's on a one-hour delay. Someone, somewhere, taps in a code number and this thing explodes an hour later. I suppose that was a feature originally put into the design to allow someone to set up the device, activate it and then get out of danger before it went off."

The Executioner looked back down at the nuclear bomb in front of them. There was a red light on in the upper right-hand corner of the setup. "And I suppose that red dot means activation has already taken place?" he asked.

"It does," Hoffman said.

"How long ago?" the Executioner asked.

The man sitting on the ground's face was still gray. "There's no way to tell," he said. "No exposed timer."

"Then the only thing for us to do that makes sense is get out of here," Bolan said, rising to his feet and reaching back down for the scientist.

But Hoffman resisted the Executioner's hands. "No," he said, "you go on. You've got a better chance of making it without me."

"No way," the Executioner said, tugging the man to his feet.

Dr. Philo Hoffman's face still registered pain. "Look, Striker," he said. "Be logical about this. I've already had a heart attack. I might have another and die any second no matter where I am. You go on."

By the time he had finished his last sentence, Bolan had the doctor over his shoulder again.

"Let me down!" the nuclear expert said. "Maybe while you're gone I can figure out some way to deactivate it."

Bolan was moving as fast as he could through the thick jungle now, brushing through limbs and vines that he and Hoffman had moved to the side on their way in, and paying the price for such speed with cuts and slices across his face and hands. "Too late to play that card, Philo," he said. "You've already told me it's a twenty-thousand-to-one shot."

The bomb had not yet detonated when they stepped out of the jungle onto the edge of the island. Bolan laid Hoffman down on the ground and pulled his satellite phone out of his blacksuit to contact Grimaldi, who was already flying back to the island in the Beechcraft. As quickly as possible, the Executioner updated his pilot.

Grimaldi understood the urgency of the situation. "ETA is ten minutes, Striker. Get the flares out and lit in five."

"I'm on it," Bolan acknowledged, and cut the connection.

He looked at his watch.

They might have as much as forty-five minutes or so left before the nuke detonated.

Then again, this might be the Executioner's and Dr. Philo Hoffman's last few seconds on Earth.

"Stay here," he told Hoffman, then ran to the end of the landing strip to begin setting the flares to guide Grimaldi in for the extraction attempt.

BOLAN HAD JUST LIT the last of the flares when he heard the Beechcraft approach. Grimaldi wasted no time landing the small plane, and the wheels barely stopped moving before Bolan lifted Hoffman into the plane and jumped in behind the scientist.

"We're on our way," Grimaldi announced as he accelerated down the runway and climbed steeply into the darkness.

Philo Hoffman was slumped in his seat as Bolan turned to check on him. The scientist was smiling yet again.

"I don't think I'm going to make it," the man with the goatee and mustache said.

"Nonsense," the Executioner said. "We're not that far from Nassau. We'll get you—"

Hoffman shook his head. "I'm not going to last," he said. He tapped his chest. "I can feel it. Right here." He tapped again.

Bolan remained silent.

"I'll tell God hello for you, and what a good job you're doing for Him," Philo Hoffman said.

Grimaldi turned slightly in his seat, the Beechcraft now cruising comfortably. "You're a scientist, Hoffman," he said. "I didn't think any of you guys believed in God."

Hoffman's familiar smile spread across his entire face. "The big bang had to come from somewhere," he said. Then he closed his eyes and his arms fell to his sides.

The smile, however, stayed on his face. A face that was no longer gray, and even seemed to glow.

The Executioner, however, wasn't smiling. There was still more work to do on this mission, and he intended to get it done. In addition to that, things had just turned personal. He had liked Philo Hoffman. And the eccentric little scientist had died in the service of his country every bit as much as any soldier, sailor, airman or Marine.

His death would be avenged.

Suddenly, an explosion sounded behind them and the Beechcraft rocked back and forth, rising and falling, then rising in the air again. When they had leveled off once more, Bolan looked over to Grimaldi. "Talk about your big bangs," the pilot said. "Looks like we barely got out of there in time."

Bolan nodded and the two men were silent for the rest of the flight to Nassau.

9

Marlin Morgan didn't even know that his old friend Harry Drake and the other former elite soldiers were in the house until they entered his bedroom.

Drake had stood just to the side of the door, watching the spectacle in the bedroom somewhat in awe, before he led the way into the room. As he'd predicted, Morgan was dressed in a sequined blue jumpsuit, his hair fluffed out and combed back just like Elvis. It had to be a wig. Morgan had put on weight like the King had during the past few years, too, and a gigantic belly now stretched against the fabric of his costume.

Marlin Morgan stood at a microphone, shouting out "Jail-house Rock" at the top of his lungs. Two women—one a beautiful blond Caucasian, the other a lithe dark-skinned black woman—lay on the round, oversize bed in front of the amplifier plugged into the microphone. A huge crystal disco ball, hanging from the center of the ceiling, twirled dizzily, casting spots of colored light first in one place, then in another.

"I told you the son of a bitch was nuts," Drake whispered over his shoulder, then stepped into the room with his Ruger .22 leading the way.

O'Hara was closest to the door, and he flipped the switch that turned off the disco ball. The flip of another switch brought more normal lighting to the room.

Morgan had stopped singing and gyrating as soon as the men had come through the door. Now, he reached behind him and turned down the CD player, then shaded his eyes with one hand. "Harry?" he said when his sight had finally fallen on Drake. "Is that you?"

Drake was surprised to be recognized after all these years. Especially considering the vast amounts of consciousness-altering substances he knew Morgan had put through his system. So he was taken aback for a moment before he finally said, "Yeah, Marlin. It's me."

Marlin Morgan stepped away from the microphone. Either not registering or ignoring the gun in Drake's hand. He shoved his own hand forward and said, "Give me some skin, old bro!"

Drake shook his head in wonderment, then shifted the Ruger to his left hand and let Morgan lead him through some complicated handshake ritual he'd seen kids do before.

Morgan stepped back and said, "Hey, you guys want some blow?"

"Maybe from the chicks," Bundy said.

Drake turned to see the former SEAL staring lustily at the two naked women on the bed, and the former Green Beret sergeant knew he'd better shut down that line of thought immediately. So Drake turned to the two women, and with his left hand put a sound-suppressed .22 into both of their foreheads.

"Far out!" Marlin Morgan yelled at the top of his lungs as his mouth dropped open. "Hey, let me do it!" He reached for Drake's Ruger.

Drake slapped him across the face with the sound suppressor and knocked him to a sitting position on the floor. Morgan looked up at him in bewilderment, a trickle of blood leaking out of the corner of his mouth. But at some level, the strike had forced the realization that something was going wrong with his evening.

"What is it you want, Harry?" Morgan asked.

"The money in your safe, Marlin. That's all. But as you can see—" he pointed toward the bed with his .22 "—we're very serious about getting it."

"I'll make you a deal," Morgan said, grinning like the madman he had become as he pulled himself back to his feet.

"I'll open the safe for you if you'll let me shoot them." He looked back to the two women again.

"They're already dead, Marlin," Drake said.

"I don't care," said the lunatic dressed as Elvis. "I'll pretend they aren't."

Drake shook his head in amazement again. "Fair enough," he said. "But first you open the safe."

Morgan rose to his feet with surprising agility and walked to a bookcase built into the wall. He pulled out the last book on the lowest shelf, and the case began to rotate ninety degrees.

Through the opening on the left, Drake saw the safe and the combination lock built into the door. He indicated that Morgan should walk to it.

Morgan strutted forward, back into his Elvis identity. When he reached the safe, he took off his huge steel-rimmed sunglasses and fished a small pair of reading glasses out of a pocket in his jumpsuit. Twisting the dial first one way, then another, he opened the door.

Stacks of money, held together in the center with brown paper bands, were revealed. Morgan returned the reading glasses to his pocket and put his sunglasses back on. "Take whatever you need, Harry," he said in a low, lusty voice. "Now, give me the gun and let me shoot the girls. Okay?"

"Wait until my men have the money out and counted," Drake said. "It'll only take a second."

Marlin Morgan looked like a hungry little boy who'd just been told that dinner was still an hour away as he stood against the wall next to the safe and pouted.

In the meantime, the rest of the men began pulling the stacks of bills out of the safe, counting them, then dropping them into duffel bags they'd brought along for just that purpose. While they did that and Morgan waited impatiently against the wall, Drake reached into his pocket for his pill bottle. Shaking out four Lortabs and a quartet of Xanax, he managed to swallow all eight pills dry.

All of the men but Whitlow watched him take the pills as they counted the money, disapproving looks on their faces.

Screw 'em, Drake thought. In another couple of days, he'd be rid of them for the rest of his life. And Whitlow would be the only one he was sad to see go. Whitlow. His right-hand man. Whitlow, who didn't pass judgment on him for taking his medications.

When the money had been counted and packed in the duffel bag, Whitlow finally did look up. "A little over two million, Harry," he said.

"Good," Drake said. "Always better to have too much than too little." He watched Marlin Morgan push himself away from the wall and walk forward, smiling. "Now I get to shoot them, right?" he said.

"Wrong," Drake said. "I changed my mind, Marlin." He lifted the Ruger and squeezed the trigger.

The .22 round caught Morgan in the middle of the forehead. The impact blew the Elvis wig off, and the man who fell dead on the floor had only a few stray strands of hair running across the top of his head.

"Nice shot, Harry."

It was Whitlow's voice, and Drake turned, holstering his Ruger and smiling at the compliment. The smile turned into a look of bewilderment not unlike the one Morgan had demonstrated earlier when the men had first entered his bedroom.

Whitlow had his own Ruger aimed at Drake's head.

"What the hell?" Drake said.

"We've talked it over and taken a vote," Whitlow said. "I'm sorry about this, Harry. I really am. But you're too far strung out on those pills and the whiskey to trust anymore. All the cops would have to do to get you to talk would be throw you in a cell for twenty-four hours without your dope. You'd be rolling over on the rest of us to get out of a parking ticket if it meant they'd give you a few pills."

"Whit, please—" Drake started to plead.

Whitlow pulled the trigger, and Harry Drake was the fourth

person to die in Marlin's bedroom with a .22-caliber hollow-point round to the brain.

Sal Whitlow holstered his Ruger. "He really was a great sergeant at one time," he said to the other men as they began lugging the duffel bags out of the room. "And I really did hate doing that." He knelt next to Drake's corpse and began going through the man's fatigues. He found the address book he was looking for in a rear pocket of the BDU pants, and a small notepad on which Drake had recorded the time and place where he was to meet Alexi Kudinov again to pick up the second nuke.

"Shake it off," Ducket said. "We already talked about it enough. It had to be done."

"I guess so." Whitlow sighed. Then he followed the rest of the men out of the bedroom to the stairs leading downward.

And by the time they reached the front door of Morgan's mansion he had shoved any remaining remorse to the back of his mind.

BOLAN, JESSUP, SAMPSON and Wilkerson all sat in large padded armchairs in front of the President's desk in the Oval Office. The news of the day was dominated by the unexplained nuclear explosion in the Caribbean.

Just as Bolan had predicted, most were pointing their fingers at the United States. And it didn't matter that the President himself had gone on camera to say, truthfully, that America was not behind the explosion and they didn't yet know who was.

Fortunately the damage done to the nearest populated areas by tidal waves and other disruption caused by the nuclear explosion had been far less than they had speculated.

The President, seated behind his desk, was typing. "There," he said as his hand moved to the mouse and a click sounded throughout the room. "I've agreed to their terms. A billion dollars in hundreds, stacked into as many briefcases as it takes, and delivered by no more than two men, driving a pickup truck with a camper on the back. We're to get the exact location in a later correspondence."

An e-mail, from a new address called Bahamabomber@ juno.com, had been waiting when Bolan arrived at the White House, summoned by the President. It had contained only the words *Do you believe us now?*

The President started to stand up, then suddenly stopped. "I'm already receiving an answer," he said, frowning down at the screen. "Or at least mail of some kind. I'll print a copy for each of you."

The Executioner grabbed the first copy to come out of the printer. His eyebrows lowered and the skin on his face tightened as he read the words of the message. "Looks like we'll be meeting these guys in New York," he said.

Jessup had grabbed the second copy to come out of the printer. "Central Park," he said. "In a clearing with park benches arranged in a circle, halfway between the Museum of Natural History and the Metropolitan Museum of Art. Midnight tonight."

The Executioner glanced at his wrist. He had been up all night, flying back to the U.S. with Philo Hoffman's body. They had stopped first at Stony Man Farm, then taken a chopper to the White House that morning.

Going without sleep was nothing new for Bolan, however, and now, in the late afternoon in Washington, D.C., he still felt sharp, restless and ready for action.

As the rest of the men picked up copies of the e-mail from Bahamabomber, the phone on the President's desk suddenly rang. The Man lifted it to his ear. "Yes?" he said. As he listened, he picked up a pen and scribbled on a piece of paper. "I'll tell them. Goodbye." He returned the receiver to its cradle.

"The FBI called," the President said. He was looking at Bolan as he spoke. "The only sets of prints they found at Ms. Brady's apartment, besides her own, of course, didn't belong to anybody named Frank."

"Then I take it they did ID him, though?" Bolan asked.

"They did. Harry Melvin Drake. U.S. Army Master Sergeant, retired. They got so many of his prints they felt confident that he had not only been there, but that he had searched the apartment just like they were doing. He was looking for something. Any idea what?"

"Anything that would grab your attention and differentiate him from the other crank calls and e-mails that come in," Bolan said. "It turned out to be the secret Brady e-mail address. It must have been written down on something Ms. Brady took home with her from work."

The President looked down at his desk and shook his head in disgust. "That's a violation of all policy," he said.

"Yes," Bolan agreed. "But people—even good people like Lucille Brady—violate policies all the time."

"I suppose so," said the Man.

Before anyone could speak again, the phone rang. "Yes?" the President said once more. There was a short pause, then the Man said, "Interesting. Very interesting. I'll pass this on, too. Ask them to send me a picture of that man, will you, please?" He hung up.

Looking up at the Executioner once more, the President said, "Memphis PD worked a multiple robbery-homicide case this morning at the estate of some eccentric rich guy named Marlin Morgan. They found him, all dressed up like Elvis Presley, and two nude women dead with .22-caliber bullets in their heads. He had a safe hidden behind a bookshelf in his bedroom. The door was open, and the safe was empty."

Bolan waited. There had to be more.

"They also found another man killed the same way," said the Man. "He was wearing OD BDUs, and had a .22 pistol with a sound suppressor on the end in a holster around his waist.

The Executioner frowned. It sounded as if the fake Iranians were encountering their own internal problems. He hoped so. That could only work in his favor. But he was still curious as to what this had to do with former Sergeant Harry Drake, who appeared to be the leader, or at least part of, this gang of phony Iranians.

"Now, here comes the interesting part," the President said.

"The homicide detectives rolled the man's prints and entered them into the AFIS system. Want to guess who the guy in green was?"

"Harry Drake."

"Bingo," the Man confirmed. "But can you make sense of any of this?"

"I can give an educated guess," Bolan said. "I've suspected for some time that these guys were short on money for something big. That *something* turned out to be two small nuclear bombs. Stolen when the Soviet Union fell, no doubt. They needed the one that went off in the Bahamas to prove they could do it. The second one is to hold over your head so they can get their billion dollars." The Executioner reached up and scratched the stubble on his chin. "I suspect Drake ran short of however much money he needed to buy both bombs and had to settle for one." He paused to let the President take it all in. "Somehow, he knew about this Elvis lover and knew the safe would be an easy score for the rest."

"Then why is he lying dead on the floor next to the rich boy?"

"Your guess is as good as mine on that, Mr. President," Bolan said. "Some kind of internal squabble would be my guess. But what matters is that this last e-mail from the group tells us they're still together, either have or will shortly have the second nuclear device and plan to carry on with the extortion scheme without Drake."

The computer clicked and the President looked down. He dropped back down in his chair again, then motioned for the other men to come around to his side of the desk as he clicked the mouse.

A photograph of a middle-aged man in green BDUs with a small round hole in his forehead looked back at them lifelessly from the screen.

The President lifted the phone and tapped a button. "Would you locate Ms. Brady, please, and send her in?" He hung up again.

The mousy little woman, whose loneliness had been exploited, had to have been close by because a knock sounded on the door a few seconds later. "Come in, Lucille," the Man said.

Lucille Brady entered the Oval Office timidly, her eyes on the floor. It was obvious that she was still ashamed of the way she'd been used.

"Lucille," the President said in a kind, fatherly voice, "I'm sorry to have to do this, but I need you to come around here and tell me if the picture you see on the screen is Frank. But I want to warn you first—this man's been shot, and he's dead."

Lucille Brady shuffled across the carpet. The men standing around the President opened a path for her, and she stepped up to look at the screen. A second later, she burst into sobs as tears began to run down her face.

It was the only confirmation Bolan, the President or any of the other men in the room needed.

Bolan turned to the President. "Sir," he said, "if you'll excuse us, we've got work to do."

"What can I do to help?" the Man asked.

"Get us a billion dollars, a whole bunch of briefcases and a pickup with a camper," said the Executioner. "And give the NYPD commissioner a call. In the meantime, we're going to fly on to Manhattan and set things up. With any luck, this should all be over shortly after midnight tonight."

The President nodded his head. "You know," he said, "I suspect you're the only man in the world I'd trust with a billion dollars."

But Bolan didn't hear him. He and the rest of the men who had been with him during this mission were already out the door and headed down the hall.

DRIVING A PICKUP THROUGH certain areas of Central Park wasn't easy during the day, let alone at night. Of course, compared to the nighttime landing Grimaldi had pulled with the Beechcraft when he'd extracted Bolan and Philo Hoffman from the island, the Executioner figured he had it easy. Turning in at the Metropolitan Museum of Art, he had guided the Toyota Tundra along a driveway through the park as long as he could before having to pull off and make his way around trees and bushes. He stayed on footpaths whenever possible, but almost wedged the vehicle between tree trunks on several occasions.

Bolan had no doubt that whoever had picked this site for the payoff had taken into account the difficulty a pickup and camper would have negotiating the sharp twists and turns on the way to the clearing. He wondered if it had been former Green Beret Sergeant Harry Drake. Maybe. Or maybe whichever of his men had shot the retired NCO had come up with the whole plan. That didn't matter now, though. What did was the fact that the Executioner was finally about to meet these thieves and murderers masquerading as Islamic terrorists. And, one way or another, it would soon be over.

Bolan mentally amended his last thought. There was only *one* acceptable way for this to end. With him still in possession of the billion dollars and the extortionists in custody.

Or, preferably, dead.

A clearing appeared ahead, and Bolan saw several park benches arranged in a circular pattern. Two lights, high atop steel poles, provided a muted illumination for the area. Bolan glanced over to Rick Jessup, who was riding shotgun and looking at a map of Central Park with the aid of a small penlight.

"This has to be the place," the DEA agent said.

Bolan nodded. He pulled out of the trees just far enough to be easily seen, flashed his headlights three times, then killed the engine. As he waited, his mind flew back to the hectic arrangements that had been made that afternoon.

The plan was fairly simple. Both Bolan and Jessup were wired with transmitters provide by the New York City Police Department. And their words, as well as those of the nuclear extortionists, would be picked up at various spots around Central Park's perimeter, where even now hundreds of well-armed plainclothes officers were positioned.

As soon as the Executioner ascertained that the men they were about to meet had the second nuclear device with them, he would work the code word "elephant" into the conversation somehow.

At that point, the police would converge on the clearing from every angle.

It would be Bolan and Jessup's job to make sure the bomb didn't go off while the police pounced.

They had been sitting there in the pickup for less than ten seconds when the door to his side opened and the Executioner turned to see a 1911 Government Model .45 aimed at his head. Glancing back over his shoulder, he saw that Jessup's door was open. The DEA man was in a similar situation. The only difference was that the pistol pointing at his head was a Browning Hi-Power.

"Get out," a voice growled behind a black ski mask.

The Executioner raised his hands and got out of the truck.

The man in the ski mask was no fool. He wore black, gray and white urban-camouflage fatigues and stayed well out of Bolan's reach, stepping back and away from the Executioner as Bolan closed the door behind him. "Now turn around, put your hands on your head and interlace your fingers," the man demanded. He sounded like a cop. Or at least someone who might have pulled security police duty in one of the branches of the military.

Bolan did as he'd been instructed. He couldn't afford to take chances at this point. Not until he had seen the nuke and determined whether or not it had been activated like the one in the Bahamas.

The man behind Bolan crept forward, quickly finding his Desert Eagle, Beretta 93-R and the folding knife. But his search was thorough, and he also brushed across the transmitter wire beneath the Executioner's shirt.

"What's that?" the voice behind Bolan demanded.

"Suspenders," the Executioner answered. "Helps keep my pants up."

The remark got him a sharp jab with the .45 in the spine. A second later, the man in the mask had ripped his shirt open and torn the transmitter and wire from his body. He called over the pickup to whoever it was who had pulled Jessup out of the truck. "Check for wires!" he said.

"Already found 'em!"

Bolan frowned. There would be no calling in the cavalry with the code word *elephant* now. From here on in, it would be up to him and Jessup to handle the entire mission.

Alone.

Four more masked men now stepped out of the foliage and went to the rear of the camper shell. One of them reached out and tried to twist the handle. "It's locked!" he called out.

"What did you expect?" Bolan heard Jessup say on the other side of the truck. "There's a billion dollars in there. Wouldn't you lock it up?"

Bolan heard a thump and Jessup let out a quick groan.

"The keys are still in the ignition," the Executioner told the man guarding him.

One of the men at the rear of the Toyota hurried to the driver's door, which was still open. He reached in and pulled the key ring away from the ignition. As he passed the Executioner again in the semilit clearing, he picked through the keys for the one to the camper shell.

A moment later, the rear door to the camper rose. Two men each pulled out a briefcase, opened it, then closed and tossed it back into the camper. Randomly picking two more, they did the same, spot-checking to make sure they weren't getting the same "magazine treatment" Bolan had given them when they'd tossed Sarah Ann Pilgrim out of the Cessna. Finally satisfied, one of the men turned toward the man holding the .45 on the Executioner. Rather than speak, he simply nodded.

The man behind the Executioner poked him in the back with the .45 again. "Nice job, catching that little princess in midair, by the way," he said. "That was you, wasn't it?"

"It was," the Executioner said.

"Well, I hope you at least got a good feel on the way down," the masked man said. "Because it's very likely to be your last."

Bolan didn't dignify the comment with a response. Instead,

he said, "Okay, you can see we've fulfilled our end of the bargain. Now, give us the nuke."

"We'll have to take you to it." The man behind the Executioner laughed softly. "Get in." With the barrel of the .45, he prodded Bolan to the end of the pickup. Jessup appeared on the other side and both men were forced into the camper on top of the numerous briefcases. Their guards climbed in after them, while the rest of the men squeezed into the Toyota's front and back seats.

The driver had as much trouble negotiating the twists and turns of the park as Bolan had. But a few minutes later, they arrived in another clearing. This one, however, had no benches.

What it did have was a helicopter.

Bolan glanced at the two masked men. They still had their pistols trained on him and Jessup. Both were close enough that the Executioner knew he could disarm one of them before he got a shot off. But would Jessup follow his lead fast enough to keep them both from getting shot by the other man? He couldn't be sure. But the real reason he made no move was not the handguns.

He still didn't know where the nuke was, or whether it had been primed to go off.

Seconds later, Bolan and Jessup were pulled out of the camper shell by their guards. The other four men dressed in black-and-gray camouflage began transferring the money from the back of the pickup to the helicopter.

"We still haven't seen the bomb," Bolan said.

"And you aren't going to," said the man still training the .45 on him. "It's at another location, primed and ready to blow as soon as I enter the code number into this thing." He reached into the breast pocket of his fatigue blouse and pulled out a remote control. Replacing it, he said, "But I don't plan to blow it right away. I'll just leave it where it is for now. Who knows how long a billion dollars will last a group of high rollers like us?" He cackled out loud, sounding like a rooster. "I might just need to come back and renegotiate another deal with you sometime in the future."

Those last words were the ones the Executioner had been waiting for. The nuke was not here, he knew now; it was at some other undisclosed location. It was primed and ready to be set, and no doubt had the same one-hour delay system built into it so these masked men could be far away in their helicopter when it went off. Even if they didn't detonate the nuclear bomb today or tomorrow or the next day or year, the nuke—which could be hidden anywhere in a city of eight million people—would hang over New Yorkers' heads like a guillotine from now on.

Bolan's hands were still raised in the air. He watched the man with the .45—who had relaxed enough now to stand at his side rather than behind him—in his peripheral vision. As soon as the man blinked, the Executioner went into action.

Pulling a ballpoint pen from his shirt pocket, he thrust it forward toward the hole in the ski mask with all of his might. The sharp steel tore through the masked man's closed eyelid, obliterating his eyeball and entering his brain. Bolan cupped his palm over the end of the pen and pushed again, driving it yet deeper until all that could be seen of the writing instrument was the very top of the stainless-steel end cap.

The man in the mask was dead on his feet. Bolan ripped the .45 from his hand as he started to fall.

Turning, the Executioner saw the guard with the Browning Hi-Power next to Jessup. Jessup had been looking away, and hadn't seen what had just happened. But the guard had, and he was about to put a bullet in the DEA agent's head.

Bolan thumbed the safety on the Government Model pistol and pulled the trigger, sending a 230-grain slug from the barrel into the head of the man with the Browning. He dropped even quicker than the phony terrorist who had gotten the pen to the eye.

By now Jessup had clued in as to what was going on. He dropped to the ground, grabbing the Hi-Power as he nodded to Bolan.

The Executioner dropped to the ground where the man who had guarded him lay, dead on his back. Rolling the man over, he found the Beretta, the Desert Eagle and the folding knife jammed into the back of the man's fatigue pants. He jerked them out, replaced them in their holsters and turned back to the fight.

The four masked men who remained on their feet had concealed themselves in the bushes by now. Occasionally, a wild shot rang out, but it was always followed by the sounds of movement, so Bolan didn't waste time or ammo returning the fire. When thirty seconds had finally gone by in silence, he called out, "Hey! Can you guys hear me?"

"We hear you!" came a reply. Then the sound of movement again, so the Executioner couldn't pin the man down by the direction of his voice.

"Then listen!" Bolan yelled. "The whole park is surrounded by New York's finest. There's no way you're getting out of here!"

"Oh, really?" came another voice. "Can any of them fly?" The words were followed by several laughing voices, then the sound of the speaker and the rest of the men changing their positions in the brush again.

These men were, indeed, well-trained warriors. The shame of it was they had been trained by America.

"All we've got to do," Bolan yelled, "is call in a few NYPD planes or choppers. They won't have any trouble following you."

"Well, we won't have any trouble pushing the button to nuke New York, either," a voice yelled back. It had come from the Executioner's right, in the bushes. When he didn't hear the man move, Bolan aimed three shots at the sound. The Government Model .45 bucked in his hand.

Then a scream came from the bush, and a man wearing urban fatigues fell out face-first.

"That dumb shit never did have the sense God gave a goose," another voice muttered. The man behind it was smart enough to move, and the rest of the .45's magazine emptied itself into the grass somewhere inside the foliage.

"THAT DUMB SHIT NEVER DID have the sense God gave a goose," Sal Whitlow muttered, then quickly moved to his right through the bushes. And it was a good thing he had, Whitlow realized, as several rounds of pistol fire tore through the leaves where he'd been hidden just a second earlier.

That damnable Cooper—again. Drake had immediately hated the man the first time he'd encountered his work. Whitlow had looked at him more like a player on the opposing team in a football game.

But now he has learning to hate the man, too.

On the bright side of things, however, the former Green Beret corporal thought, Cooper was putting money in Whitlow's pocket. Cooper had just killed Felix Bundy. Whitlow hoped Cooper would kill a couple more of his men before he died himself. The only problem was that while each dead man raised the shares of those who remained, each death meant one less gun to fight Cooper.

And Sal Whitlow certainly didn't relish the idea of facing this mysterious warrior man-to-man.

Besides, there wasn't going to be enough time to let Cooper kill off all the rest of the men before Whitlow took out him and his little friend. He suspected that Cooper's warning about the NYPD officers circling Central Park was more than bluff, and NYPD certainly did have enough planes and helicopters at their disposal to follow their own chopper until it just flat ran out of fuel if need be. They had found the transmitters wired to Cooper and the other guy's chests. That meant that whatever code word they had agreed upon wouldn't ever get to the regular cops backing them up.

But the police surrounding Central Park would hear the gunfire, and even though hearing gunshots in Central Park at midnight was hardly anything new, the sheer amount of fire would eventually bring them running.

And while Whitlow knew he was a damn good fighter, he wasn't prepared to take on several hundred well-armed cops. If he was going to get out of this mess, he needed to do it fast.

For a second, the former Green Beret considered just turning around and making a break for it, away from the clearing. The urban-camouflage fatigues in which he was dressed were not so different than the clothing NYPD's Emergency Rescue Squad wore, and he still had one of the badges that he'd taken from a dead security guard back at Marlin Morgan's place. He had always been a smooth talker, and chances were good that if he discarded his mask, he could bullshit his way through the lines and be gone before the perimeter cops even knew he was one of the men they were looking for.

Whitlow kept perfectly still, hidden by the darkness, as well as the bushes and trees, as he considered this strategy of retreat. The problem was that fleeing would mean leaving all of those briefcases full of money where they were—some already in the chopper, the rest still in the camper shell. And over the months it had taken for him and Drake to work out this plan, then recruit the rest of the retired elite fighting men they needed to help them, he had begun to think like a rich man. By now he had reached the stage where he couldn't imagine living the rest of his life on an Army pension or getting another job.

If he didn't get the billion dollars, Sal Whitlow decided, he would just as soon die.

So the man who had once served his country so honorably— the same man who had turned criminal after leaving the U.S. Army and even murdered his old sergeant and closest friend— pulled the almost-empty AK-47 magazine from his rifle and shoved a fresh box of 7.62 mm rounds into the carriage. Flipping the safety to autofire, he aimed the weapon at the Toyota Tundra and held the trigger back. He was careful not to fire into the camper shell itself for fear of damaging the brief-cases and money still in there. He avoided the gas tank, as well—burned money didn't spend. But his rounds punched holes in the pickup's windows, doors, the roof of the camper and the ground below it.

All four tires blew almost simultaneously, and the pickup dropped a good half foot closer to the ground as he swung the full-auto Russian assault rifle back and forth.

Whitlow dropped the empty magazine and shoved in another fresh box. He had caught a glimpse of movement on the other side of the truck during his long burst of fire. It had looked like a patch of denim—probably blue jeans—shifting to the side when the tire next to the patch had exploded. He could still see the blue denim in the semidarkness, so he switched the AK's selector switch to semiauto, aimed and fired at the faded blue target.

A yelp of pain came from the other side of the truck, and Whitlow grinned. It had to have been Cooper's little sidekick. He had never actually met Cooper, or even knew what American law-enforcement agency employed him. But what the man had done so far to block their progress told Whitlow a lot about him. He was big, strong, tough, fast and smart. And you could probably subject him to the most horrendous tortures men had ever dreamed up over the centuries and never get the satisfaction of hearing him yelp or exhibit any other sound or expression that designated pain.

Still moving through the bushes to change position after every volley he fired, Whitlow heard the sounds of the remaining men on his team acting similarly. The unfortunate thing about it all was that Cooper and his friend were on the other side of the pickup, behind the engine block, and while the heavy rifle rounds were destroying the vehicle they had no punch left by the time they'd made it through all that steel. Add that to the fact that they were all trying to avoid blowing up the Toyota—with roughly half of the money still in it—and the superior numbers they had over Cooper and his sidekick didn't amount to squat.

Sal Whitlow knew there was only one thing to do if he was to get out of this alive with the money. He had to somehow make his way through the foliage, around to the other side of the pickup and camper. By now, the police who had encircled Central Park would be making their way toward the gunfire, code word or not. But they would be moving slowly and cautiously—none of them anxious to give up their life on this operation about which they probably knew little more than what was necessary to play their roles.

If Cooper had told them there was a nuke involved, at

least half the cops would have probably called in sick, grabbed their families and headed for the nearest highway out of New York City.

So, as quickly and silently as possible, Sal Whitlow let the other men continue shooting as he began to creep in a wide circle around the pickup.

The answer to his problem was actually fairly simple.

He just needed to get into a position from which he could shoot Cooper and the other man in the back.

AS SOON AS THE Government Model .45 had run dry, the Executioner dropped it and drew the Beretta 93-R from under his left arm. From behind the pickup, he had a clear shot at the helicopter. He had seen the silhouette of a pilot inside the glass bubble earlier, but now the man had evidently dropped to the floor, out of sight.

That mattered little to Bolan. He was more interested in the chopper than the man who flew it.

Taking careful aim at the blades above the helicopter, the Executioner squeezed off a single round. A loud ding sounded above the sound-suppressed cough as the bullet struck its target and bent the blade. Lining up the Beretta once more, Bolan damaged the other blade, as well. Then he switched the 93-R to 3-round burst and sent two trios of 9 mm slugs directly into the windshield. The bullets didn't break the glass, but they sent spiderweblike cracks crawling completely across it.

There, Bolan thought as he holstered the Beretta and pulled the big Desert Eagle from his hip. Let them try to fly the billion dollars away in *that*.

The Executioner pushed the huge .44 Magnum pistol's safety switch to the fire position. It would be louder than anything else that had been discharged so far in this gunfight, and that might prove to be a psychological advantage. Even if it didn't, the huge weapon was loaded with RBCD Performance Plus Platinum cartridges. These ultra-high-performance bullets left the barrel hundreds of feet per second faster than normal .44 Magnum ammo and produced a total energy transfer once they met any water-based target.

Like a human body.

A sudden burst of fire sounded from the bushes, and the Executioner raised his eyes—and the Desert Eagle—just over the hood of the pickup. He fired a lone, blind round but knew he'd missed the man hidden within the leaves when he heard a shuffling sound.

Other fire came at the truck from different spots in the thick foliage. Bolan took note of the irony of the situation. Here he was, in the middle of Manhattan Island in New York City, New York, fighting the same sort of fight he had fought so many times in the jungles around the world. The fact was, it was little different than when he and Philo Hoffman had attempted to defuse the nuke on the small Bahamian island. Dark, with plenty of concealment if not actual cover. And the moon was almost full, allowing for more light than usual but also giving the whole situation the same creepy feel the island had held.

A burst from another AK-47 drove the Executioner back down behind the engine block where Jessup was changing magazines in his Glock. The two men had been forced to stick close together behind the pickup's engine block, and were getting in each other's way almost as much as the men who were firing at them.

Bolan ducked back down again as DEA Special Agent Rick Jessup turned to lie flat on his belly and fire around the flattened tire in front of him. When return fire came his way, the young man rolled back behind the engine block.

Round after round after round continued to pepper the pickup.

Bolan had dropped to his knees again to avoid the onslaught. But while his Desert Eagle rested, his brain went into doubletime. They were outnumbered. By how many men, he couldn't be sure. But they had lost their communication with the police around the perimeter, and while the Executioner knew those men would eventually be drawn to the gunfire itself, they would come too late.

He and Jessup would have to save themselves.

The Executioner turned and saw the thick bushes and trees ten feet behind him. Then, turning back to Jessup, he said, "Can you keep things hot while I try to circle them?"

Jessup nodded. "I'll do my best," he said. "But I'm running low on ammo."

Bolan reached up and drew the Beretta 93-R from his shoulder rig. "Take this," he said as he jerked the extra magazines from under his other arm. "Unscrew the suppressor. This is one time we'll need the noise."

Jessup took the pistol and magazines. "Keep your head down," he said.

Bolan saw him flip the Beretta's selector switch to 3-round-burst mode. Then, as the DEA agent rose to fire blindly into the bushes, the Executioner dived back away from the pickup and into the concealment of the leaves.

He was slightly surprised when he drew no fire. That had to mean he hadn't been seen by the men on the other side of the pickup.

Once in a while, he thought, a person actually caught a break.

Of course, that didn't help him determine where his enemies were hiding. The Executioner would have to find that out on his own.

Slowly and cautiously, Bolan began to duck-walk through the bushes and trees of Central Park. Each step brought a cracking sound beneath his combat boots as they crunched the dried and dead leaves beneath him. But there was no way to avoid that noise. He would have to try to time his steps with covering gunfire.

The Desert Eagle was gripped firmly in the Executioner's right fist as he stepped, waited for more gunfire, then took two more steps until a break in the explosions came again. While visibility had been fairly good under the moon when he'd been behind the pickup, inside the thick growth surrounding the clearing it was diminished to almost nothing.

Suddenly, the hair on the back of the Executioner's neck

began to itch. Although he was almost in complete darkness, he instinctively reached forward and felt his hand hit the side of a rifle barrel. He pushed the barrel to the side as whoever was holding it pulled the trigger.

Bolan felt the rifle barrel heat up as a half-dozen 7.62 mm rounds blew from the barrel of an AK-47, flying wide past the Executioner. At the same time, however, Bolan felt the Desert Eagle drop from his hand as a fist came down on top of his wrist. He reached over and grabbed the AK with his other hand, trying to wrench it from the unseen man, who also now held it with both hands. But his adversary was strong, and Bolan's movement sent both of them rolling through the bushes.

Sharp twigs and thorny vines tore at the Executioner's hands and face as he and the other man rolled. Bolan relaxed his grip slightly, letting his attacker pull the rifle closer to his chest. But the movement had been calculated, and it also drew the Executioner's arms closer to the man's face. A split second later, Bolan twisted and swung an elbow into his opponent's chin.

The man's grip loosened on the rifle. Bolan jerked it from his hands, but before he could turn it on his opponent, the man punched his forearm again and the assault rifle went flying off into the darkness.

The wrestling continued, with both men trying to get the upper hand. At one point, the Executioner freed his right hand and directed a right cross down at the man's chin. But by the time the punch reached its target, they had started to roll again, and Bolan's big fist barely grazed the other man's skin as it drove on into the dried leaves covering the ground.

Somewhere in the back of his mind, the Executioner registered the fact that dozens of voices could now be heard in the distance. The NYPD cops stationed around the perimeter had finally received their orders to close in. But they weren't going to get there in time to help Bolan.

As usual, the Executioner was on his own.

Bolan and his attacker finally rolled out of the bushes into a small clearing, and the Executioner took note that just like the other men he had seen, this man wore urban-camouflage BDUs and a black ski mask. The front of the mask had been soaked with sweat and spittle from the exertion of hand-to-hand combat, and the two eyes stared out at him, filled with hatred.

The two men continued to wrestle, coming up onto their knees. The man in the mask suddenly screamed at the top of his lungs, then jerked away. Reaching behind him, he pulled out a black-coated Ka-bar combat knife with a seven-inch blade. Bringing it high over his head, he sliced it down through the air toward the Executioner.

Bolan leaned back, letting the knife pass in front of him less than an inch from his face. At the same time, he reached for the folding knife on his belt and flicked the blade open with his thumb. Using his left hand to momentarily pin the knife hand of the masked man to his chest, the Executioner drove the blade to the hilt, through the bottom of the mask and into the center of the man's throat.

The man in the ski mask froze as if he'd suddenly turned to ice. But before Bolan could even withdraw the blade, he lifted his hands and the Executioner saw a remote-control device in one of them.

The same type of remote-control device that could be used to prime a time-delayed nuclear weapon like the one in the Bahamas.

Bolan ripped the blade to the side, severing the man's carotid artery before withdrawing the bloody steel.

The terrorist fell backward onto the ground. Bolan grabbed the top of the ski mask and jerked it from his head. Pulling the penlight from the pocket of his blacksuit, he shone it down into the dead face.

What he saw didn't surprise him. In addition to blue eyes, this fake Iranian had dyed black hair. The blond roots were clearly visible, especially at the part. This man had wanted no questioning the fact that he was an Islamic terrorist from the Middle East.

But none of that seemed important now. The big question was, had this man somehow found the time and opportunity to push in the code to initiate the countdown sequence of the second nuclear bomb? Bolan stooped and pried the remote control from the man's dead fingers. He used the penlight again to look at the face of the instrument.

There was no way to tell.

A strong flashlight beam suddenly illuminated Bolan and a voice shouted, "Don't move!"

The Executioner looked past the light to see two plainclothes NYPD officers. One held the light and a pistol. The other covered him with a 12-gauge riot gun. Bolan still had the folding knife in his hand when Hal Brognola suddenly appeared between the two men. He had pinned his badge to the lapel of his sport coat, and the well-chewed cigar stump stuck out from between his teeth. "Lighten up, boys," the big Fed said. "He's one of the good guys."

Another man wearing a suit stepped up next to Brognola, and Bolan recognized him as the NYPD commissioner. They had crossed paths a couple of times before, and now the commissioner nodded in acknowledgment to the Executioner. Then he turned and shouted, "Listen up!"

At the sound of his voice, all conversation in the clearing ceased.

"Everybody except the officers with the prisoners get back out into the woods," the commissioner ordered. "And quit contaminating the crime scene!"

As the men began to disperse, Bolan looked past Brognola to see that two men wearing urban camouflage BDUs had been taken into custody alive. Their hands were cuffed behind their backs, the ski masks had been ripped from their heads, and officers were shaking them down, finding a variety of hideout knives and small guns.

Bolan stepped in closer to Brognola as the officers with the shotgun and flashlight turned away. "We've still got a problem on our hands," he whispered to the Stony Man director of sensitive ops.

"Did he arm the bomb?" Brognola asked.

"I don't know, and if it's like the one Dr. Hoffman and I found on the island, there's no way to tell except on the bomb itself."

"Do you know where the bomb is?" Brognola asked.

Bolan shook his head. "It could be anywhere."

Brognola practically bit his cigar in two.

"Get hold of Jack," the Executioner said. "Tell him to show up here with a chopper as fast as he can." He glanced at the helicopter he had ruined earlier in the fight, wishing now he had left it alone. The pilot was obviously a coward who flew but didn't like to fight. And the Executioner could have made good use of the helicopter now.

Rick Jessup suddenly appeared holding both Bolan's Desert Eagle and the Beretta 93-R that had been loaned out to him. He handed the weapons to the Executioner, who holstered them and then walked over to where the two prisoners stood. "They clean?" he asked the cops who has just finished searching them.

The cops nodded.

Bolan reached behind the closer man and grasped the chain between the two cuffs. Pulling up on it, he saw the man wince as he guided him toward the helicopter. "Grab the other guy, Jessup," he said, and the DEA agent made the last man cry out in pain as he lifted the other handcuff chain.

Bolan drew the Desert Eagle again just before he opened the door to the helicopter. Aiming both the big .44 Magnum pistol and the penlight inside the chopper, he found exactly what he'd thought he'd find.

The pilot lay on the floor just behind the seats. He had already taken off his ski mask, and immediately said, "Joseph Manson Knox, formerly of the queen's Special Air Service. And I surrender." His hands were held high over his head.

Bolan put the light back in his pocket and pulled the man out with the same hand. Jessup stepped forward and cuffed him.

Now that he and Jessup had the three remaining fake Iranians isolated, Bolan holstered the Desert Eagle and pulled the folding knife from his belt again, flipping it open. Blood from the man he had wrestled with still stuck to the blade, shining a spooky crimson under the moon. Holding it up so the three men in handcuffs could see it better, the Executioner said, "As you can see, this blade's already had a workout on one of your men. Who was he?"

"Whitlow," said one of the men in cuffs. "He's been in charge ever since—"

Bolan interrupted him in midsentence. "We'll get the whole story from you later. Right now, we don't have time." He reached into another blacksuit pocket and produced the remote control. "Do any of you know if Whitlow had set the wheels in motion yet?"

All three of the captives shook their heads.

"Do you know where the bomb is?" Bolan asked.

"Yeah," said one of the prisoners who wore his hair in a flattop. "But let's start talking about deals first. I want someone from the district attorney's office to promise, in writing—"

Bolan threw his second right cross of the night. Instead of crumpling leaves, this one knocked the man unconscious and dropped him to the ground. The Executioner turned to the next man. "There's *his* deal," he said. "Yours is going to come with this." He stuck the needle-tipped knife just below the man's nose and pressed it into the skin until a small trickle of blood appeared. "Do you want to tell me where the nuke is?"

Before he could answer, the helicopter pilot spoke up. "No need for that," the former SAS man said. "I know, and I'll take you to it. I'll even fly you there if you'll provide me with another aircraft." He glanced up at the warped blades of his helicopter. "It appears you've broken mine."

Almost as if he'd been listening to the conversation, Jack Grimaldi suddenly appeared in the sky flying a McDonnell Douglas Defender helicopter. A second later, Bolan's satellite phone rang. "Yeah?" he said into the instrument.

"Get the rest of those guys out of the way for me, will you, Striker?" Grimaldi spoke into the Executioner's ear. "I'm about to land."

Bolan called for several police officers and pointed to the unconscious man on the ground and the man he had pricked with the knife tip. "Take these two into custody," he said. "I'm taking this one with me." Now he pointed at Knox.

As Grimaldi landed, the Executioner looked to the man in the urban camouflage who was still standing. "When you get to your cell," he said, "get down on your knees and thank God that there were all these cops around you tonight." He paused, then added, "I work a little differently when I'm alone."

The man took note of the inference, and the knowledge of just how close he'd come to death caused a lump the size of a baseball to form in his throat.

A few seconds later, Bolan, Jessup and Joe Knox were lifting off in the Defender.

Epilogue

Grimaldi set the Defender down in a parking lot in the Bronx, only a few blocks from Yankee Stadium. Bolan, Jessup and Knox all sprinted down a sidewalk, then up the steps of an ancient brownstone apartment building to the third floor, where Knox—still cuffed—nodded at a door with the numeral 8 tacked to the rotting wood.

"It's in there," the former SAS pilot said. "We were all here when Scott set it up."

"Who is Scott?" the Executioner asked.

Knox shrugged. "One of the guys you killed, I guess," he said. "At least someone did."

"You got a key?" Jessup asked.

Knox shook his head.

"I do," the Executioner said, lifting a black combat boot and kicking the aging door so hard it cracked into two pieces as it swung open. With the Desert Eagle leading the way in case there were more of the phony Iranians guarding the bomb until the last minute, he raced inside the seedy apartment.

The apartment had bare brick walls and wooden floors in almost as bad a shape as the door. It was empty of all furniture, and had obviously been rented by the original leader—Harry Drake—simply to serve as a place where the nuke could be hidden.

Among other things Bolan had learned from Knox during the flight, Drake had been killed by Whitlow at Morgan's Memphis mansion. It had been Whitlow who then brokered the deal with a former Russian Spetsnaz operative named Alexi Kudinov for this second nuclear bomb.

The Executioner dropped to one knee beside the nuke and saw the red light shining in the corner of the face. The apparatus looked exactly like the one he and Dr. Philo Hoffman had been forced to leave behind in the Bahamas.

Which meant that, yes, it had been activated before Bolan had killed Whitlow. And Bolan, Jessup, Knox, Grimaldi and millions of New Yorkers had somewhere between one second and one hour before they were all vaporized.

Bolan had told Grimaldi how the system worked during the flight from Central Park to the Bronx, and now the pilot and Knox looked down and saw the red light.

"If a nuclear specialist like Hoffman couldn't disarm the other one," Grimaldi speculated, "what kind of chance do a couple of amateurs like us have?"

"Not much," the Executioner replied.

"Well," Grimaldi said, "we sure don't have time to go looking for another lab geek and hope he can do differently with this one."

"No, we don't," Bolan agreed.

He turned to Knox. "Is there a kill code?" he asked, pulling the remote control out of his pocket again. "An entry I can make to counteract the primer?"

Knox was shaking with fear, his eyes glued to the bomb. "I think there was," he said. "But I don't know what it is."

Bolan had no doubt that the terrified man was telling the truth—Knox didn't want to be blown into oblivion any more than the next guy. So the Executioner leaned down and lifted the nuke into his arms, cradling it almost like someone might carry a baby. He found the device surprisingly light. "Let's go," he said. "We don't know how much time we have. But we've got to try to get this thing out of here and away from people."

The three men sprinted back down the steps to the sidewalk, with Grimaldi drawing his S&W Model 66 .357 Magnum revolver to cover Knox while Bolan carried the nuke. Few residents of the surrounding buildings were out on their porches in the wee hours of the morning. But those who were had stared at them when they'd run past a few minutes earlier. Now, with a gun and some strange-looking object also on display, they stood up and began hurrying back into their own homes.

When they reached the Defender, Grimaldi pushed Knox into the backseat, then slid behind the controls while Bolan climbed quickly up next to him. Stony Man Farm's top pilot gave the chopper the minimum amount of warm-up time. But each second seemed like an hour.

Finally, the Defender rose into the air and headed off across the Bronx toward the Atlantic. Bolan turned to glance at Knox. The former SAS man had let himself get out of shape, and he was still panting from their last sprint from the apartment. But the discomfort he was experiencing from the run was overcome by the fear Bolan still saw in his eyes.

As they rose higher into the sky, the shoreline finally appeared, and then they were over the Atlantic. Grimaldi nursed every bit of speed he could manage out of the Defender as they sailed over the dark waves below. The pilot constantly monitored the gauges in front of him, as well as referring to a hand chart he'd produced from somewhere and kept in his lap.

After what seemed like an eternity, Grimaldi turned to Bolan. "We're far enough out now," he said. "Unless there's a ship in the area."

Bolan pulled his satellite phone from a pocket of his blacksuit and tapped in the number to Stony Man Farm.

"Hal already called me," Kurtzman told Bolan. "Give me your coordinates."

Bolan leaned over, consulted a gauge in the control panel in front of Grimaldi and read off their latitude and longitude. A second later, he heard typing, then the click of a mouse button being pushed. Then Kurtzman said, "All clear of water traffic below, Striker. Get rid of that thing and get out of the way!"

Bolan opened the door and dropped the nuke into the darkness.

Grimaldi immediately spun the helicopter around 180 degrees and headed back toward New York, still flying at top speed to get away from the blast that was certain to come.

Ten minutes later, they heard a muffled boom behind them.

All three men breathed a sigh of relief, then Knox leaned forward. Now that the nuke had been safely disposed of, the Briton had found his voice again. "Could you take these handcuffs off now?" he asked, addressing Bolan. "It's obvious I'm not going anywhere, and you wouldn't have ever found the bomb without my help. After all, I *did* help you save eight million people."

"Well," the Executioner said, "that's one way to look at it. The other way is that if we hadn't interfered, you were more than willing to let eight million people die in exchange for your cut of the money." He turned in his seat to watch the man's reaction.

Joe Knox nodded and fell silent, realizing his pleas were falling on deaf ears.

Bolan turned back to Grimaldi. "There's a Russian named Alexi Kudinov who deserves a little attention, I think," the Executioner said as the helicopter made its way on through the darkened sky, back toward New York City.

James Axler
Outlanders®

SHADOW BOX

A new and horrific face of the Annunaki legacy appears in the
Arizona desert. A shambling humanoid monster preys on human
victims, leaving empty, mindless shells in its wake. Trapped inside
this creature, the souls of rogue Igigi seek hosts for their physical
rebirth. And no human—perhaps not even the Cerberus rebels—
can stop them from reclaiming the planet of their masters for
themselves....

Available May 2009 wherever books are sold.